Just A Hint Of
Fantasy

Works By

TARA HENDERSON

IZZY THORPE

ALLISON MATALONE

ROCHELLE SANGABRIEL

JILLIAN NETHERLAND

K.I. RUNYON

AMANDA KENNEDY

Cover Design by Izzy Thorpe
Book Design by Izzy Thorpe

This edition is published by Ingram Spark

ISBN 979-8-9891436-0-3 PRINT
ISBN 979-8-9891436-1-0 EBOOK

Cover design by Izzy Thorpe
Book Design by Izzy Thorpe

Table of Contents

CONTENT WARNING-
Be advised of the following:

Alte by Allison Malone may contain gore and bodily harm.

The Seven Devils by K.I. Runyon contains themes of suicide, self-harm, and sexual assault.

Introduction

Story offers us respite from the everyday demands of life. When we open a book, we're granted instant passage from our own station in life to countless others with only a trip to the library or bookstore. We can visit places and characters filled with adventure, excitement, and intrigue. From chapter one we step through a door and get the chance to cozy up to another life, another place, another reality altogether.

But what if the latest thriller, sci-fi, or romance novel failed to whisk you far enough away? What if you wished to escape further still?

What you're searching for is fantasy. Until you've stepped into the pages of fantasy, you've yet to experience the limitless worlds behind those covers. Worlds rich with creatures unheard of, magical wonders, and the supernatural. What better way is there to tune out the noise of the world than from within an entirely new one? Fantasy has the power to pull you along on unimagined adventures, introduce you to characters from someone else's dream world, then lay before you a reality unrestrained by the rules of yours.

Within these pages are ten fantastical stories dreamed up by seven kindred authors. A group of writers who have gathered for years to hone their crafts, tell their stories and encourage each other to take risks on the page. For their first anthology, The Kindred Writing Collective has opened the doors of fantasy and woven for you tales spun with devils, hosts, magic, sirens of the sea, and more.

Welcome to your temporary escape. Step inside and look around. And, aside from enjoying the well-crafted tales of fantasy, delight in being among the very first to become acquainted with the promising new authors of The Kindred Writing Collective.

The Crows

Izzy Thorpe

◆

One for sorrow.
Two for mirth.
Three for a funeral.
Four for a birth.
Five for Heaven.
Six for Hell.
Seven for the devil, his own self.
    - Counting Crows, old nursery rhyme

Adelaide had never seen a lion, yet lions were the thing that haunted her dreams. It had been a lion on the flags that came when Euliss had been called to war. They were great, black beasts that reared their might atop fields of red, billowing in the wind. The lion's visage was painted across rows of iron breastplates that shuddered with every step. And when the Báron leading his army unraveled his parchment to read Euliss' name, Adelaide saw a beast pretending to be a man. On the little finger of the hand holding the parchment spelling out her husband's fate, gleamed a silver signet ring with a lion's form stamped in the middle. Adelaide had never seen a lion, yet lions were the thing that stole the man she loved.

Adelaide had wanted to fall to her knees and beg the Baron to leave her husband be. But the fear of the beast's eyes catching hers was too great. She had heard the stories of monsters in the form of men that swallowed women like her whole. She shuddered at the thought of the Baron's tongue against her skin, the lion's teeth biting deep into her flesh. So as Euliss was called to war, Adelaide had cowered, pinned down by her own helplessness. How was she supposed to face a lion?

All she could do was pray that Euliss would make it safely back home.

The crows came to her shortly after Euliss had gone. They flooded her porch steps like spilled ink and she traded her food scraps for their company. Adelaide had heard that crows were bad omens, but still she could not bring herself to shoo away her winged visitors. Instead, she welcomed them, happy to have something to share her woes with. Each day she sat on her steps and waited for Euliss to come home to her, and each day it was only her crows that came.

They brought her small gifts, offerings of friendship. Adelaide would find things such as stands of ribbon or coins waiting for her on her porch. She talked to the crows and it seemed like they understood her, nodding their small heads like birds do as she spoke. She expected them to leave when the weather changed, but they stayed through the chill the autumn air brought.

When Adelaide heard the news that Euliss had died in the war, part of her died too. Her husband was gone and she was alone in this world. The crows gathered around and watched her as she wept, great waves of tears spilling out of her. Adelaide sobbed and waited in vain for a man who would never return home.

In her dreams, it was a lion that tore Euliss apart, the mighty beast surrounded by fields of black and red.

As the days grew colder and shorter, the nip in the air reminded Adelaide that she should be preparing for the season's change. The harsh winters before had been difficult to survive with Euliss by her side, but now that he was gone it would be even harder for her to stay warm and fed. Food grew scarce, but still she gave what she could to the crows. Still the crows brought her little gifts.

Adelaide had thought she had cried enough when Euliss had died, but when her bleeding stopped and her belly began to swell, she soaked the earth with her tears once more. The crows gathered around her in solidarity, and Adelaide imagined that they understood all of her fear and pain. She imagined they understood how she worried that the life growing inside of her could be taken in an instant, just like the life that had helped create it.

Now in her dreams, it was a hand that haunted her. It wasn't just any hand, the hand in her dreams, it was one wearing a signet ring on his little finger, the lion's form catching in the light. The hand reached out from the dark and snatched the babe away.

When the letter came from the Baron offering Adelaide a marriage she flew into a rage. The Baron had said he could use a third wife, he claimed he would take the baby in as his own. He hunted his prey with words like 'pity' as his weapon. Adelaide threw the letter on the ground and the crows descended upon it, tearing into the parchment and shredding it apart. Even the Baron's lion wax seal was not spared from their vicious beaks. Still Adelaide's hands shook with fear.

Time passed and the crows bore witness to Adelaide's growing stomach. It was as if she had swallowed a stone, the weight inside of her was so great. One day the crows brought her a patch of sour grass and Adelaide knew that the babe inside her would be a boy. She wished that she could grow wings like the crows and fly far, far away with them, somewhere the Baron would never find. She would fly high enough that a lion's paw could never reach to swat her down. But she could not avoid her encroaching fate that gathered around her like the falling snow, whatever it may be.

On the day that Adelaide gave birth to baby Euliss, named after her husband, she was alone. The labor had been such a shock, the midwife didn't have time to make it to their farm. Even the crows had not yet arrived. Adelaide thought she would split in two and nothing would put her back together again. When she held little Euliss in her arms, all she could think about was the fear of having him taken from her.

Adelaide had never seen a lion, but she heard that they were mighty beasts. She heard that one swipe of their massive paws could fell a dozen men and one mighty roar could shake the knees of an army. They were the thing that had haunted her dreams and stolen her husband. Hunched over her babe, so new to the world, Adelaide tried and failed to think of ways to defeat a lion.

When the crows came to visit her and her new babe, they came in a flutter of excitement, feathers drifting around. They had never ventured inside her home before, but now they flowed in through the window. Blood dripped from their beaks and their talons. They turned her floor into a field of black and red, feathers and blood. One crow stepped forward, walking all the way over to Adelaide and up next to the babe cradled in her arms. The rest of the flock shuffled in close.

Despite the blood, Adelaide was not afraid. Instead, she lowered her bundle so that the crows could see little Euliss. The babe's eyes grew wide, their blue depths filled with wonder at the sight of his new flock. Blood dripped from the crow's beak leaving splotches on his blanket, but Euliss had made his way into this world through blood and pain. He was not afraid either.

The crow began coughing and retching, exciting the rest of the flock into a frenzy. Before Adelaide and her new babe, from its depths the crow bestowed its gift. A bloody finger sat before them, a little finger with a silver signet ring. A lion felled upon a field of black and red.

Adelaide no longer feared that her babe would be taken. She no longer dreamed of lions.

She Woke to the Smell of Salt

Tara Henderson

***

Sabrina stared into the vastness of the stars for hours, remembering the constellations her parents had taught her. Her favorite being Delphinus the Dolphin, who carried the Greek poet, Arion, safely away from his enemies. It seemed like a lifetime ago that she was with her family, when in reality it had only been a few months. If only Delphinus could have been there that night to keep her safe.

The waves rocked the fisherman's skiff as she gazed into the sky until finally, she settled into a dreamless sleep. It was her favorite kind of sleep, void of surprise monsters, sturdy nets, and excruciating pain.

She woke to the smell of salt, fish, and the sea; the cocktail she was born from. Taking in the smell, eyes still closed, she let out a long sigh. Last night's restlessness was going to make for a long day at sea.

Faint light peaked over the horizon, and she squinted her eyes open. The yellow light of the sun broke through the morning clouds and shimmered off the blue ocean as the sky shifted from dark blue to a pink glow.

Her thoughts turned to her current situation. Was she to blame? Her family might say yes. They had lived in these waters for generations, watching the townsfolk from afar as babies were born and grew: first into children, then into teenagers, and eventually into fishermen. Her people's lifespan is many times longer than theirs, so they grew accustomed to the faces of the locals and watched as family legacies unfolded. In a small town like this, there were many dark secrets that, of course, everyone knew.

She heard a fisherman begin their morning chores around the docks, but she remained cozy in the skiff with her thoughts, not yet ready to face the day.

Her people heard the silence that fell over the town the day Charles's wife died trying to bring their second child into the world. The baby didn't survive either. That day was twelve years ago, by human timing. Jack had been six years old – too young to lose his mom.

His wife had been part of the Eridanus family, a family that had been in these parts since the town began. Some amongst Sabrina's family even claimed that the Eridanus lineage began in the sea.

Sabrina had watched Jack for years before the switch. He was different from the others – quiet and pensive. He had the look of someone who had been transformed by their past, forever set on a road towards sadness, because he was that person.

A seagull swooped overheard and landed on the skiff next to hers. Her people teach that seagulls are messengers of changing times and tides – oh how right they were.

Every summer, when Jack was out of school, he would spend hours alone on the shore, near the rocks, close to Sabrina's home. Her parents warned her to stay away, said that when humans are allowed to see that which they don't understand, they can't help but to take advantage. She had thought they were exaggerating. How much harm could a small human boy cause?

Humans tell stories of her kind, and at the same time, claim that they don't really believe in them. But last night, when Sabrina approached the docks, the night security guard trembled when he saw her eyes. The eyes always gave her away. Her family pod is known for having gold irises with green pupils. Sabrina's eyes did not change when she became human. She was grateful for that, to have a piece of her family with her.

The guard stepped aside and let her climb aboard the skiff even though harbor rules prohibited sleeping on boats. June was the only time warm enough for her to sleep on the water like this. Even with the quilts she nabbed from Charles' house, she still had goosebumps.

She wiggled her toes and stretched her legs, still amazed by the sensations. She propped herself up against the chair and saw that fishermen were already swarming the wharf like orcas around a school of herring. Some were pulling anchor and others preparing nets. The largest of the ships was still loading ice, ignoring her presence in one of the five skiffs bobbing behind it, ready to be towed out to sea.

She noticed Charles walking towards the docks, like he did every day just after sunrise. *He never once changed his routine, not even the morning after she showed up on his porch. She blamed herself for not seeing Jack's trap. But once he cast the net, and snatched her pearl, their future was decided.*

After writhing in pain for hours, next to her capture doing the same, she accepted her situation. She realized that she only had one option. She did not have to say a single word to Charles when she arrived. He looked into her eyes, draped a blanket around her naked body and let her inside.

Nautical décor hung on his walls, covered in years of dust. She could tell that the once bold colors were dull. There was mermaid art jammed into every nook and cranny, breaking up the blue stripes and whitewashed walls. The mermaids, unlike everything else, didn't have any dust. Charles touched one and explained that the day Jack's mother died was the day that he received his first mermaid figurine.

During the three months known as tourist season Charles charged triple for the 'local' experience. It was her first summer as a human and Charles treated her as if she'd been his assistant since his first day out on the boat. He boasts to his customers that he knows all the secret spots to catch Rockfish and Mackerel even though it wasn't until Sabrina joined him that his online ratings went up and people didn't grumble about paying the fee for his expertise.

She taught him to read the ripples on the water to determine which fish were below. He picked it up quickly and the other guides were all annoyed at him for taking more than his fair share of the summer business.

She pulled on her fleece, shoes, hat, and raincoat, damp from sitting in the skiff all night, then walked over to Charles's boat.

"G'mornin, Sabrina."

"Hello, Charles."

"We've got a full boat today. Guests'll be here in an hour." *Charles never once asked Sabrina what happened to Jack. It's almost as if he knew. Jack's stacked books of mermaid lore never raised Charles' suspicions until it was too late. That first week that they lived together, Charles was all business.*

He explained the nuances of town life, brought her onboard the boat, and even gave her his late wife's clothes. She was learning that was the way of these hardened sea-loving humans. They moved on quickly, or at least most of them did. But not Jack.

Over the next hour they prepped the boat, the grocer delivered the meals for the day and their guests arrived. Her heart felt at ease as soon as they left the harbor. The wide expanse filled the empty parts of her, the ones left desolate when Jack caught her in his net and stole her pearl.

The waves were harsher out here, forcing the motor to fight for every inch forward. Early morning seagulls were specks in the distance, waiting for them to return home so that they could chase the fish entrails that would be tossed overboard.

About twenty miles from shore they stopped, set the hooks in the water, and ate their breakfast.

"Lucky for you, Tracy's has the best breakfast burritos this side of the Mississippi," Charles said, followed by one of the many jokes that he repeated each trip.

The guests laughed on cue.

As morning turned to afternoon, Sabrina noticed Charles watching the water again. While she agreed to teach him to spot Striped Bass and Bluefish, she refused to teach him how to find her people. Even if she had, he would probably never see them. They knew better than to be spotted.

Sabrina doubts that her family was as kind to Jack as Charles was to her. They knew exactly how he had joined their world when he showed up wearing her pearl. They knew that she would never give it up freely, no matter how much the human world fascinated her. Once the switch happens though, it cannot be undone. Like her parents had warned, humans can't help but to take advantage.

Jack being new to the ocean world, was not as careful or as skilled at remaining hidden like her people were. They had seen him twice already. Each time she heard Charles stifle a gasp. Their clients never noticed his reaction. Jack stayed underwater, bound by old magic. Because he stole her pearl, he would never be able to raise his head above the surface of the water. She saw it in his eyes. The regret. The self-loathing. He knew what he had done was wrong. He tried to get as close to humanity as he possibly could, but he would never be human again.

Alte

Allison Matalone

◆

The taste of one's own flesh should be unpleasant.

Daetric finds it spongy, tough, and slightly salty from sweat, which is the only indication of his nerves. The already severed skin at the base of the ring makes it easy to slip his teeth in and pull. The skin is pliable; the difficulty is tearing. Once he rips a strip free, blood streams from the wound, and he sucks it down, his mouth sealed on the finger. He doesn't want to make a mess.

The pain is within his threshold; he breathes through his nose evenly, and focuses on why he is here. As long as he can remember that, he can withstand any trial or tribulation that may come.

One of his canines scrapes roughly against the metal ring secured on his forefinger, sending a tremor down his spine. He resolves to be more careful, and he gingerly eats around the ring.

A bead of sweat gathers at his temple and falls, trickling down his bare chest and thigh. Circled about him are the rest of the *Sicarius Sodality*; the shrouded figures only remind Daetric further of his nakedness.

◆

"It's symbolic," Adept Tarek had explained on one of their many walks during the last three years of his novitiate. "When you are born, you come into this world nude and new. This will be your rebirth into our order. You must be bare to receive the blessing."

Daetric had nodded.

"There is one other thing." Adept Tarek had held up his hand, tugging the glove off, revealing his Death Finger. It was devoid of skin and muscle, held together through magic and the Santric ring it bore.

"You must also make the sacrifice. The method you choose will dictate the faction you belong to." He held up three fingers. "*Imus* Sect deals with villages and some small cities, Iatro with the larger cities and the militaries, and then there is.."

"*Alte*." Daetric's eyes shone bright. "You're an *Alte*,"

"Correct, the Alte Sect's duty is to protect everyone on the continent from those in power."

"I am ready, Adept, whatever my choices."

"I have a feeling, dear boy, you will choose the most difficult path."

And he did. At the beginning of the ceremony, Adept Tarek towered over him as he was given his options, laid out on a plank between them.

"Now is your choice. First: by my hand." He indicated a knife, the handle made of finger bones, its blade black with rivets of red. This would be the quickest method. "By theirs." He gestured toward a pot of flesh-eating insects, which would be the slowest method. "Or by your own means." He held his hands out towards Daetric.

Daetric met his mentor's eyes. "I choose my own means."

Tarek nodded and lifted a finger, and the plank was removed.

"Daetric has made his decision," Tarek announced to the assembled men. "By his own means, he shall join the *Alte*." He twisted his *Santric* ring, working it off his forefinger, his mouth a grim line, with only a slight twitch of pain in the corner. Once it was free, he slipped the ring onto Daetric's finger.

It took all of Daetric's training and stubborn stoicism to keep his face stone and his knees from trembling. Even as it tightened, pressing deeper and deeper, constricting blood to the finger — even as it cut into the skin, severing veins and muscles, stanching the blood flow, and then melting the skin below, until it was just the warm metal against the bone and base his knuckle – even then, he kept his face still.

———— ◆ ————

As he works his way to the knuckle, nibbling at stray strands of muscles, he lifts his eyes in search of his mentor. But Adept Tarek fades into the sea of shadow cloaks, all with their hoods pulled down.

Death Fingers point at him, some a dull phlegm yellow edged in brown through age, others gleaming white in the firelight. The old hands, and new, in this trade of death. In the low light, their fingers remind him of twigs.

———— ◆ ————

Daetric and his siblings would play Keeper of the Peace in the woods behind their family's farm. Aeron, the oldest twin, used to tie a twig to his finger, he would be Justice, and Jaemin, the younger twin, would be the Evildoer, and the rest of the children — Gaeml, Raelin, and Daetric — would be the victims.

Jaemin, the Evildoer, would spin a wild tale about all the cruelty he would do, his brown eyes dancing and his face twisting into smirks and sneers. And the younger siblings would run into the woods and hide, hoping the Evildoer would be caught before he found them.

If Aeron, Justice, caught the Evildoer and poked him without anyone seeing, he would win, ending the reign of tyranny. If the Evildoer found all of the others first, he would win.

But sometimes, Jaemin would find everyone except Daetric, and Aeron wouldn't be able to get Jaemin without anyone seeing, either. Eventually, Aeron would give up and declare Jaemin the winner.

And only then would Daetric come out. It was during these times that Daetric would privately declare himself the winner. He was always the best hider.

It's why he survived.

It was dark, and Aeron was shaking him and Gaeml. Jaemin stood at the foot of their bed, holding Raelin's hand.

"Want to play Keeper?" Aeron asked.

Gaeml squinted up at his brother. "But the wolves are out."

"We'll play inside."

They never played inside.

"Where's Father and Mother?" Raelin asked. Under one arm was the doll Father had crafted for her. Mother had been trying to stop her from sleeping with it now that she was ten winters old.

"They're playing too, Rae," Aeron said. "They are going to be the Evildoers. They're outside, counting. Jae and I are both going to be Justice. How does that sound?"

"Wait." Daetric reached under his pillow, pulling out string and some twigs. "You need Death Fingers."

"That's right, Dae, we do." Aeron held out his finger.

Above all about that night, Daetric remembered Aeron's fingers trembling as he tied the twig on his brother's finger.

———— ◆ ————

As Daetric makes his way past the second knuckle, the skin is closer to the bone, harder to catch between his teeth. He moves his finger to the side of his mouth and begins to gnaw.

———— ◆ ————

Daetric darted from his room before anyone else. He knew where to hide. He'd been cleaning the fire pit earlier in the week, and he had heard a sound up the chimney. Looking up, he'd seen a bird make its way up and out of the chute. How did it get there? he wondered. He easily found places for his hands and feet in the stone as he climbed just a little way up. There he discovered a cubby, where one roof beam had been cut too short; inside was a half-built nest. It was the perfect spot for a small eight winters child. He crawled in, and to his delight, he could look out through the paneling to the main room.

Daetric spied his brothers, standing in the front room; they stood side by side. Both looked more like Father than ever, despite being only ten and three winters. Then Aeron placed three fingers over his heart and bowed his head. Jaemin followed suit. Why were they praying? That was when Daetric knew this wasn't a game.

Shouting came from outside, and then the clash of steel and a woman's cry. Aeron pulled two of Father's swords from the wall and handed one to Jaemin.

The door shattered; a burly man strode in, blood dripping from his sword. On one side of his head hung a half a dozen or so bones that clicked together with every step. They were of different lengths, but all were narrow, and at the bases were black rings.

Aeron and Jaemin swung clumsily at the man. Their thin arms could barely lift their swords, and each swing was slow and easily deflected. The man laughed as each blow became slower. Finally, he knocked Jaemin to the floor and buried his sword in his stomach.

Aeron let out a howl and slashed his sword, catching the man by surprise and slicing his face from eyebrow to chin.

The man roared and brought his sword across Aeron's throat.

A cry sounded from across the room. It was Gaeml. He was always so restless and curious. He must have heard the fight and come to investigate. He charged at the man with his wooden practice sword.

Daetric shut his eyes and stuffed his hand in his mouth and bit down as hard as he could. He didn't want the man to hear him, nor did he want to see any more of his family die.

He could hear the man stalking through the house; he knew from the shrieks when he found Rae. And he knew from the silence when she was dead.

He stayed there for what felt like hours, watching that man sit on his father's chair and eat his family's food. The bodies of his brothers lay at his feet.

Daetric may have dozed at some point, but he jerked awake at the sound of voices. His legs were cramping and he desperately wanted to straighten them out but he was afraid of making any noises.

The new man's back was to the chimney. He had on a long fur cloak with a hood. Daetric strained his neck trying to catch a glimpse of his face. He spoke in the language of the North, all hard consonants.

The burly man slurped from a cup and answered in the same language. The man in the cloak pulled a coin purse out of his pocket and tossed it on the table.

And then they were both gone.

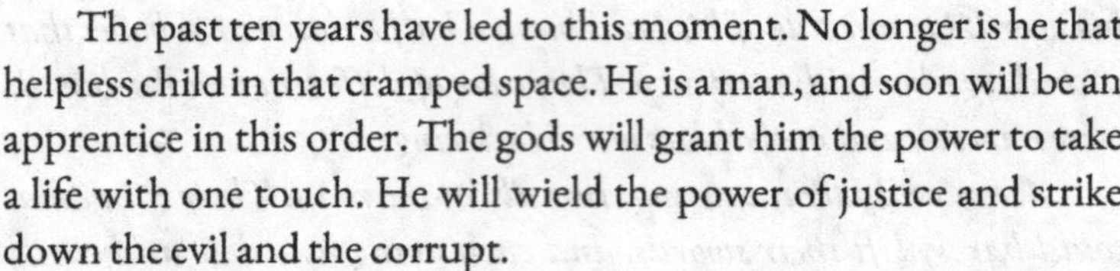

The past ten years have led to this moment. No longer is he that helpless child in that cramped space. He is a man, and soon will be an apprentice in this order. The gods will grant him the power to take a life with one touch. He will wield the power of justice and strike down the evil and the corrupt.

For five hundred years, the *Sicarius Sodality* have been tasked with keeping the five kingdoms at peace. They bend the knee to no king; they are an impartial observer until needed. Now he, too, will don a shadow cloak and learn the art of being an assassin.

Daetric tears the last bit of flesh from the pad of his finger. He chews slowly, savoring, then swallows.

The taste of one's own flesh should be unpleasant. But as the power rolls through him, seeping into his pores and then down into his very bones, it is anything but.

Price of Magic

Izzy Thorpe

◆

When I walked into the office and saw the splatters of blood coating the walls, I was reminded of my constant desire to quit. There's no way I was getting paid enough for this. I only took this job because Stephanie was my friend, and I always thought the whole 'blood, sweat, and tears' thing was more of a metaphor. I didn't think I would have to deal with so much actual blood. With a sigh, I made my way to the back room where I knew Stephanie would be. I didn't ask what kind of animal she sacrificed this time, I didn't really want to know. Although, it must have been something bigger than before. There was so much blood this time. The janitor would probably find the remains tomorrow, but that wasn't my job. Dealing with Stephanie was.

"You promised," I said flatly, and at the sound of my voice Stephanie looked up like an animal caught in a trap. "You promised that you wouldn't do this anymore," I repeated.

Her eyes found mine and I could see the rising mania that was starting to take hold. The sight made something in my chest clench, like I was witnessing an accident in slow motion that I was powerless to stop.

Stephanie sat in the middle of the floor with hundreds of sheets of paper strewn about her in a circle. Some were crumpled into little balls and others had smudges of red on them that must have come from the blood on her hands. I could see the way her hair had gotten messed up from raking her hand too many times through it in frustration and I recognized the clothes she wore as yesterday's outfit, although the wrinkles were new. Stephanie couldn't meet my eyes for more than a few seconds before looking away in shame.

"I know."

"You don't. You act like nothing is changing, but it is. You're different."

"You act like that's a bad thing. I'm getting everything that I ever wanted."

"At what cost?"

"YOU DON'T UNDERSTAND!" She shouted, her voice rimmed with a desperate edge. "I need this. I tried to do everything on my own, but I just couldn't. All of my ideas were BAD. Or even worse, mediocre! People expect things from me now."

I just stared at her in silence.

"I have a reputation!" She continued, her volume rising. "You don't understand what it's like to have all of this pressure. I'm supposed to be the best. How can I be the best with no new fucking ideas?!"

I flinched. Of course I wouldn't understand, she made sure of that. There was never any light left for me in Stephanie's shadow.

I sighed in defeat and went to sit next to her on the floor. She was trembling a bit, but still clung to me like I was the only thing that would keep her from drowning. Desperate fingers reached out for my hand then wove us together. With my free hand, I stroked her frayed curls and she slumped into my lap, drained from her outburst. She knew that I couldn't stay mad at her. This was all my fault, after all. I was the one who found the book. I was the one who thought it would be funny to try one of the rituals inside. How was I supposed to know that the old gods would actually show up? That they would offer to reshape the fabric of the world to make our wishes come true? I wanted it all to be real, how was I supposed to know it would be?

I helped Stephanie over to the cot that she kept in the corner, just for all those times she worked through the night. I waited for the steady rise and fall of her chest before going to deal with the papers. They covered the floor and I hesitated, unsure of where to start. My nose crinkled at the acrid scent of magic in the air, a mix of sulfur and vanilla. Another thing for me to deal with.

Stephanie had always wanted to be a fashion designer. She wanted the world to look up in awe at the things that she created. She wanted to be adored by her fans and hated by her competition. Anything was worth the sacrifice if it meant that she could succeed, and all it had taken was a simple wish.

I gathered the sketches from the floor and flipped through the piles. They were indeed brilliant, although some seemed a little ambitious. The looks that she had drawn played with the human form, interacting with the body like skin was also a fabric for her to manipulate. I picked up a sketch where a horn of fabric was emerging from the figure's right shoulder. The look was bold, but the balance was off. Stephanie always did have trouble getting the balance right. Using a pencil from the nearby desk, I lengthened the horn a good bit, curving it in a way that framed the figure's face. Better.

The sketches were good. They could use a bit of refinement, but getting the ideas down was always the hardest part. With these she would get the awe that she so desperately craved. I unfolded and looked through the discarded ideas, the ones that were crumpled and tossed aside in frustration. Stephanie was right, they were bad. Just variations of cliched drapings held together with ribbon. I threw those away, she didn't need them with fresh magic coursing through her mind.

◆

The first time we did the ritual, it was more of an accident than anything. We both thought it was a joke, right until sand the color of gemstones and crushed dreams started pooling at our feet. We had laughed about it, about how something so absurd could actually exist—that people would be willing to do something so wild in the hopes of getting their dreams fulfilled. 'Hard work pays off!' Stephanie would always say, but I'll confess that there was always a part of me deep down inside that believed in things like magic and rituals.

We'd gone on a post-college camping trip together, but we had both been too broke to afford anything more than renting out a cabin in the woods. The weekend was supposed to be a relaxing commune with nature before we had to face the tragedy of a working class adulthood—a little hiking, a little cooking over a fire, and a little bit of sleeping under the stars. I wanted to relax at a beach, preferably away from lots of people and Stephanie had wanted to jaunt through New York. Camping the woods was our in-budget compromise.

It was in the attic of our rental cabin, hidden amongst dusty boxes that I found the book. I told Stephanie about it when she came back from her hike and she laughed at me.

"Do you actually believe in that kind of stuff, Ash?" she had asked.

I shrugged, embarrassed, "I don't know. I just thought it would be kinda cool."

Stephanie laughed at me and at that moment I hated her. I hated her just like all of the other times I hated her because of something she did or said, but frustratingly, I loved her just as much.

"We're about to start our careers, about to be bound to the endless, hellish wheel of capitalism. This could be the last time we get to do something like this. Even if it's all just make believe." I told her. I didn't mention how much I wanted the magic to be real. How much I needed it. Stephanie frowned and walked away, effectively ending the conversation.

The next day, while I had stayed back and read, Stephanie came back from her hike with a half-dead rabbit in her arms. All she would say is that she found it, and that she'd thought about it and was willing to try the ritual.

"It can be symbolic. Like we're manifesting our futures. Sacrificing the rabbit will be like...proving how much we want this."

"Want what?" I asked.

Stephanie grinned back in response. "Go get the rest of the stuff."

She didn't have to tell me twice. I got all the supplies ready right away and put together the makeshift altar. It didn't take much, I could use items from the cabin. Then I pulled the heavy book into my lap so I could read the words aloud.

When it came time for the sacrifice, though, I couldn't do it. I held the rabbit and the kitchen knife, but it suddenly became too real, too gruesome. Never in my life had I been a bloodthirsty person. There was nothing that I had ever been desperate enough to fight for like this.

Stephanie took over and I could see the same hesitation clearly on her face. Then some wave of determination crossed her, some grim desperation, and she did what had to be done. Even as blood spilled from the rabbit's twitching body onto our altar, I was jealous. I read the words exactly as they were written. The book in my lap was cold and lifeless, but the blood soaking into Stephanie's hands must have felt so warm.

At first nothing happened, there was only silence and the rabbit's blood puddling at our knees. Then Stephanie laughed. She laughed and laughed until she had trouble breathing, even her gasping breaths echoing through the trees. She laughed until the purple smoke spilled out around us. We were filled with the sound of sand and static, the smell of sulfur and vanilla. And before us hazy forms appeared and asked why we had called on them.

"What? What is it?" Stephanie tapped her fingers against the table and her foot twitched. "If you have something to say, then just say it. I have work to do."

I had asked Stephanie to meet me at the coffee shop by her studio. It took a lot of convincing. By this point she had shut me out of pretty much her entire process.

"I'm just worried about you. Have you even slept since the last time I saw you?" She looked terrible, even more so the closer I looked. Dark circles had nested under her eyes and her fingertips were raw and peeling. Her usually wild hair was too messy even to claim she woke up like that.

Stephanie let out a sharp laugh. "What does it matter if I've slept? I'm getting my work done." She looked at me, really looked, and I leaned back away from the intensity of her gaze. "Oh, you should see it Ash, see the looks that I've made. It's like nothing that's ever been done before. This show will change everything, I know it."

I hesitated, then spoke, "I'm sure it will, Steph, but can't you change the world and still get a couple hours of sleep every now and then?"

Stephanie tried to rake her hands through her hair, but gave up halfway due to the tangles.

"It's only temporary. I'll sleep after the show. Trust me, it's worth it."

"Last time really was the last time, though, right?"

The dreamy expression she got thinking about her work dropped away. "You're still going on about this? Yes, okay? It was the last time."

After her first show, Stephanie came to me and begged for us to do the ritual again. While critics sang her praise in the papers, she sobbed her eyes out convinced that nothing she would create in the future would be as good as this. She needed the inspiration that the old gods had given her. I hesitated, knowing that nothing was ever free and the old gods had yet to ask anything of us. Even the book warned of a cost, but wouldn't mention what exactly it would be. There would be a price to pay, but Stephanie didn't care.

In the end, I agreed to do it. Of course I did, it was Stephanie asking after all. Stephanie had promised me that then would be the last time as well. She always promised, every time.

"Have you..." I hesitate again, fidgeting with the straw on the drink I ordered. "...been seeing things?" Ever since the first ritual, I had been seeing magic. I started to see it all around me, wherever I went. It was little things at first, a glimmer in the eyes, a sparkle in shadows. Innocent magic. The kind of magic that could be believed in without anything being asked in return. The more we saw of the old gods, the more magic I saw. It was like the sand was getting in my eyes, tainting my vision.

"I have no idea what you're talking about," Stephanie said. I could tell from the look on her face that she did.

"Don't play games with me," I snapped. "You can see the magic, can't you."

"Why are you getting mad Ashley? It's so pretty. The magic is all around us, all the time, and it's so, so lovely." Her features were twisted and pulled by her adoration and mania.

I thought about the magic I had seen. I saw a man with a gray tongue at a coffee shop. I asked him what he was drinking and he told me that it was coffee, black. I asked him if he ever added cream or sugar and he told me no, that it all tasted the same to him. I saw a woman who bent over to pick up a 20 dollar bill. Her fingertips glowed with luck. I saw a man who in certain light looked like a corpse and I could tell that death wasn't far behind him.

It could be considered pretty, I supposed. But more than that, it felt wrong. I felt like a voyeur to a part of the world that should have stayed hidden. My instinct when faced with the very pulse of magic was to turn away. I guess Stephanie's was to sink her teeth in.

"There will be a price. You know it just as well as I do, but you refuse to admit it."

Stephanie laughed again, that same, sharp laugh. "God Ash, do you ever fucking shut up about this stupid price? I'm doing better than I've ever done. People know who I am now. They love me. They see my work and they love me for it. Can you say the same? What have you done? Who loves you?"

I flinched and she could see that she took it too far. She stood up, defeated, and turned to leave.

"You know, we have literally anything we could ever imagine at our fingertips and all you worry about is what it will cost. How did I not know how fucking boring you were?" Stephanie turned and left, leaving me alone in the coffee shop.

We had fought before, but never like that. Before I had been someone helping her follow her dreams, even following my own alongside her. Now, I was just someone standing in the way.

After that night I found her in her studio, Stephanie worked like someone possessed. The gods had granted her what she wanted most and she reveled in it. Days passed and she stopped letting me in her studio. She told me that she wanted me to be surprised when I saw her creations on the runway for the first time. I tried to get her to eat and to sleep, at least a little, but the mania I had seen didn't leave her. The more I pushed, the more she pushed back, until we were hardly speaking at all. An eerie cloud of dark magic formed around her. She had done the ritual so many times now that the magic clung to her like a bad smell. Stephanie barely left the studio.

I knew that she was mad at me, because I was the one who made her promise to stop doing the ritual. She was addicted, anyone could see that. I knew right away that she had gone too far when I had walked in on a previous sacrifice and she had blood on her hands and guilt in her eyes.

I was standing on the catwalk, high amongst the lights and wires, ready for the show to start. There was no seat in the audience reserved for me, there never was. As Stephanie's assistant, I could have gotten something for myself if I wanted, but I preferred it up here. I felt like I could see everything. I watched as the VIPs came and sat, waiting to affirm how brilliant Stephanie was. How daring, how inspirational, how devastating to those who would come after her because no matter how good they were, they would never be better. A low whisper hovered in the air, caught in the thick anticipation.

The lights dimmed and everyone fell silent, ready to have fulfilled Stephanie's promise that tonight's show would be unlike anything they had ever seen before. Silence, then the music started. The first model emerged from behind the curtain and all eyes snapped to her. She was tall, blonde and beautiful. And covered in a black cloak that stretched from her neck all the way down. Thump, thump, thump, the music pounded as the model made her way to center stage and with a practiced hand, undid the clasp of her cloak.

The cloak spread aside, blooming like a flower to reveal the design underneath. The inside looked like the forest, wild and dangerous. A hoop skirt was woven from branches and vines with flowers and leaves bursting from the spaces between. Feathers and fur decorated the inside of the cloak. When the audience saw it, they went wild. They cheered and gasped like a good audience, their appetites whet for the rest of the show. They must not have seen what I saw.

Because for me, the skirt of branches didn't weave itself into a twisting corset. From my eyes, the branches seemed to grow into the model, wrapping itself through her ribcage. Flowers seemed to bloom right from the bone. Tulle was twisted around her spine. And while I gasped at the anatomical impossibility of it all, the audience cheered on. The model seemed un-bothered by pain, so I didn't think she felt any. She just smiled at everyone with her glass eyes and insides made from Stephanie's idea of art.

The first model left and the second one followed after. This time it was a man covered in gold. The bodice of his outfit was made of various bits of gold; coins, jewelry, and other odds and ends that grew denser as they descended until they melded into his skirts of glowing, golden fabric. No one could look away from this heaven's warrior. What must they all have thought? That the gold was attached to some thin fabric, something that blended in with his skin? Or maybe they thought it was latex, a trick of the light? The golden pieces were stuck deep into the man's skin like he was an ancient dragon that had fallen asleep on his pile of treasure. I wanted to throw up. I wanted to rush down to the stage, stand in front of this gilded object of beauty, and pluck something from his chest like fruit from a tree. Just to see what would happen.

This must have been everything that Stephanie ever wanted. I watched as her show was beautiful and brilliant, haunting and unforgettable, all at once. Another model came forward, and another. Each one flaunting a look so unique, so macabre. I bore silent witness to reconstructed limbs and reimagined bodies, each look hiding its horror with a delicate, ephemeral beauty. I wanted to scream out for the show to stop, for everything to just stop, but like the rapt audience, I was also mesmerized. I couldn't look away from the horrors parading in front of me. From my perch on the catwalk, I could just make out Stephanie standing behind the curtain, watching as she changed the world of fashion. As she changed the world. Her eyes were glazed over with euphoria and sunk deep into her skull. I couldn't tell how long it had been since she last slept, but I would have guessed days, if not weeks. Her fingers looked red and raw and at this point I wouldn't find it surprising if she literally worked them to the bone.

The next model was wearing water. For me, it was in the shape of a dragon that twisted and curled around the model, a young-looking girl with rows and rows of long sharp teeth. I wondered for the hundredth time that night what the others saw, unused to the sight of magic as they were. They hadn't slit the rabbit's throat, still thinking it was a joke at the time. A way to let off some steam. They hadn't seen the old gods appear in front of us and challenge everything that we had ever known with the time it had taken them to materialize.

"What would you have us do?" they asked Stephanie. "What is it that you desire?" they asked Stephanie. The old gods didn't even look at me, Stephanie's shadow. They saw her dreams and desires and bloodthirst for the whole goddamn world in her eyes. They didn't even see me. I thought it was just enough to witness their impossible magic. Stephanie's whole gruesome menagerie paraded below and I could see everything from my perch. No one could see me. The water girl was still on stage and her dragon-like outfit swirled around her, roaring out a heart-throbbing sound. And of course, the audience ate it right up. They cheered, clapped and hollered at the show, enlightened by it. The air was thick with magic.

I remember the old gods had asked me what I wanted when I finally tried the sacrifice on my own, what my wish was. 'I don't know,' I told them, because I really didn't. I just liked to see their inhuman forms, witness their impossible magic. They told me that I would know eventually, that there would be something that I desperately wanted. I hadn't thought so, but they seemed so sure. At last, I wanted the show to stop. I wanted to be done with the parade of magnificent horrors in front of me, but I just couldn't bring myself to look away.

The audience stood with a renewed fervor at every look. They clapped until their hands turned red. And the louder they were, the more the magic poured out of them like a fog. They kept clapping. One woman clapped so hard her hand snapped at the wrist and she kept clapping. One man's eyes turned black and bulged like a fly's. All the better to see the designs with. Despite their growing deformities, the audience hooted and hollered for more.

The audience became an immaterial thing, their shapes losing all meaning. The magic in the air turned them into dough, squishing and pulsing with the music. I watched it all from the catwalk. My attention was torn between the models and the audience. Every passing second introduced something new and horrific.

"Enough," I said aloud. Sand the color of gemstones and crushed dreams started pooling at my feet. Magic, thick like smoke, formed around me. *What would you have us do?* It was just a thought, a voice in my head. It was a cruel answer to a prayer I hadn't made yet.

"I can't watch this anymore." As soon as the words left my mouth, the wish was granted. I could no longer see the show or the audience. I could no longer see anything. It was like a switch was flipped. I was no longer under the compulsion of Stephanie's captivating abominations. Instead, I stumbled to where the door was. My hands groped the wall, looking for the door handle. The sound in the room grew to an unbearable level. All I could hear was an overpowering noise. Pushing the handle, I stumbled through the door and away from the event. When the door slammed behind me, everything went silent.

———◆———

Reporters talked for days about the fashion show that no one made it out of. The designer, the models, the audience all vanished without a trace. Some speculated things like aliens had come and abducted everyone because they liked the designs so much. Or that the show was terrible and the designer Stephanie Muñiz had hidden everyone away because she didn't want word getting out about just how bad it was. No one had any real guesses, they were all too grounded in reality to believe that the old gods had come and collected. I knew it was the work of the old gods, there was no doubt. Stephanie had asked for favor after favor and finally the price needed to be paid.

Part of me liked to pretend that the old gods too had been enamored with what they helped her create. That they were in such awe that they built a new world just for her, a place made for hollow women and golden men, and made her its queen. Deep down, part of me knew better. The old gods always demanded a sacrifice. The piper must be paid. I dared to call them forward and glance at their magic, now I'll never see anything again. They gave Stephanie everything, so she had to have everything taken away.

Stephanie had once told me that no one loved me. That I had never done anything worthy of being loved. Sometimes, I thought that she was right. I'd never created anything, not the way she did. At least I used to believe I could. Now that I was blind, how was I supposed to create anything? Do anything?

I moved on. I tried to, really. I got a low-paying job in a new city. It wasn't anything exciting, but it paid the bills. I learned how to move around the new city without my eyesight. I followed the rules. I did all of the things that I was supposed to do. Every day was the same corporate bullshit, so much so that I started to think that maybe this was the true price of magic. Like I said, I moved on. But I still remembered the ritual. I could no longer read the book, but I still remembered the words. All I needed was a sacrifice.

The Descent She Chose

Tara Henderson

◆

The final moments of sunset flickered across Blake's hill country property. She hiked in front of Henley, her mother's best friend, not sure her heart was up for another of her mom's wild adventures. Her mom had passed four and half days ago. She had left her last words in a note. Blake was supposed to get to the mouth of a cave at the moon's waxing phase. Blake had not felt like doing anything. She had never understood her mother's passion for existence and even now, with clear instructions, she felt aimless. But she trudged along this dusty path anyway.

With a heavy sigh she pushed the wild blackberry bushes aside, ignoring the micro cuts they left across her forearms. The slight chill in the air replaced the smells of earth and fauna as the dying heat of the sun ceased to magnify their scents.

Henley walked through the opening Blake had created and paused. She looked so much like Blake's mom that people often thought they were twins. Blake didn't see the resemblance, but maybe that was because their physical appearances were their only similarities. Henley was soft-spoken and sweet. Her mother had been neither of those things. As they neared the base of a small hill, the mouth of the cave appeared, dark and ominous.

"Just like the note instructed, 'past the bushes and east of the spring'," Blake said. They both approached the opening.

Blake was still reeling from her mother's passing. She wasn't surprised to find the vague note left behind – that was exactly like her mom. But she never expected the revelation of a hidden cave on their acres of Texas land. She had spent every school break exploring caves around the world with her mom, but not once had she mentioned one so close to home.

The opening wasn't more than two feet tall. It looked like a shadow. Blake had only ever glanced at this area as a kid, distracted as she was by the taste of blackberries and fresh water from the spring. Once she graduated high school she wandered around the country, picking up odd jobs, and staying as far from nature and her mother as she could.

"Blake, look." Henley pointed near the entrance. "We definitely found the right cave."

A cloud of dirt hovered lightly, suspended mere inches above the ground. Blake thumbed the iridescent moonstone pendant that her mother had left her, remembering this phenomenon from a cave in Austria. That trip was the first time Blake met her mother's caving friends, including Henley. They had said that the dirt hovering is a sign of power nearby, original power, the kind that helped to create the earth. At the time Blake thought they were messing with her.

They set their backpacks down and knelt next to the crevice. Blake ran her hands along the entrance, dusting its edges, which upon closer inspection looked more deliberately made than she would have expected.

There was so much left unsaid between her and her mother. She picked up a clump of dirt and smashed it against the entrance.

"Dammit. Why did she have to go?" It had always been just the two of them. Both of them were always so sure that they were right, that there was never any compromise. That's why Blake had left. She had to. Her mom was always so right, and so God-damned cryptic. Even in her dying words, left on a note, because she hadn't thought to tell her daughter that the cancer had returned.

Blake's mother and her friends were mysterious people, traveling the world in the name of conservation, and yet not once did she see them working with any organizations or other preservationists. Most of the time her mother had left her with her aunt and cousins here in Texas. When she did get to travel with them, they told fantastical sagas. Their favorite being a creation story that weaved together gods, creatures, and ideologies from the Native Americans, Pagans, Indian Vedas, and more.

Blake pushed herself up and opened her pack to get her gear. "Do you want to go first?" Even though she had been in a countless number of caves, and this one was in her own backyard, she felt her pulse quicken. She tried to steady her breath, but it continued to quiver.

"The journey is yours, dear. I'm just along for support. You go first." Henley said.

"Henley, do you really believe the same stories as my mother?" Blake asked as she buckled her helmet and secured her elbow and knee pads. Seeing the dust floating outside the cave had her grasping to remember all the different tales she had heard over the years.

"Of course, I do. But, Blake, sweetie, this goes past mere belief. Like me, you'll get to know. You'll understand better once you've made the journey." Perhaps Henley had one thing in common with Blake's mom after all – they loved to make ambiguous comments.

As Blake waited for Henley to gear up, she waved her hand through the hovering dirt and wondered what she was getting herself into. Did she want the same veiled life as those guardians? As her mother? As Henley? Is that what they even are, guardians? What are they protecting? Why does this all need to be a secret?

Once Henley was ready, Blake turned on her headlamp, pushed her bag in, and inched her way through the opening. She felt with her hands, more than seeing. It was impossible to look forward and crawl at the same time. The cave calmed her nerves; now she was in her element. The mystery of what was ahead made her heart beat a little faster, in the good way. This darkness is where she felt at home. There was just her instinct. Her ears heard every tiny sound, the scrape of an insect or the droplet of water. Her smell noticed more detail, earth and dampness, like Scotland after a rainy day.

After about twenty feet, she emerged into a glowing chamber. The light was similar to the glowworm caves in Alabama, blue bioluminescent sparkles dotted the cave walls like trapped constellations. Blake's breath caught in her chest with the unexpected memory. That was her first caving trip with her mom. She had been ten, still scared of the dark. Her mom never allowed her to sit in her fear though – always forcing her to face them. A good quality to have now, but at ten, she hated her mom for it. Once she saw the glowworms though, she changed her mind about the dark.

Henley emerged a minute later and gasped, "I forgot how beautiful it is."

"You've been to these caves?" Blake felt a stab of jealousy. Why couldn't her mom have shared this with her when she was still alive? Couldn't her mom have been the one to pass on this family…*responsibility?*

"The entire crew has been here. Just once though. We all visit other locations at least once, so that we know the terrain. But mostly, we stay near the caves that we have guardianship over. Mine, as you know, are mostly in Europe."

Blake was about to ask why they hadn't invited her to join them when a soft thud from behind startled her. A heavy door had covered the cave entrance. Blake tried the latch. Tugging and pushing. She shone her light on it. There were no key holes, just a series of intricate designs, patterns similar to a mandala but interrupted by drawings of insects and animals.

She almost panicked but Henley put a hand on her shoulder, "Don't bother. It will open once you have decided."

"Decided what?"

"The question your mother never got to ask you. She wanted to be the one to—."

A gust of wind interrupted Henley. Blake's hair flew into her face and through it she saw something pink flying towards them. She re-tied her hair back and focused on the object. It was an oversized butterfly, mesmerizing them both with its glowing appearance. It drew near and landed on Blake's pack. Up close, Blake recognized the pattern on its wings as the star constellation of Sagittarius. The butterfly and the archer, both powerful symbols of transformation and freedom.

"There's a story for this creature, right?" She asked. A feeling of déjà vu overcame her.

"The first butterfly emerged from Mirage, the creator of the earth.

Mirage sent her to look at the world. While the creature traveled, it flapped her wings, painting colors across the gray surface as she traveled."

Blake grasped the moonstone pendant again as understanding seeped in. Her mother's stories were true. This one about Mirage. She thought it was merely a Native American story, from the Lipan Apache tribe that settled here, in this exact valley. But it was real. Her family had passed this story down since they first arrived in the Texas Hill Country, back in 1000 AD or so.

She looked at it. She held her hand out and the butterfly landed on her, it's weight barely registering. It walked across her arm and a swirling script, that wasn't there before, began to glow, as if rising from within her skin. It read, "Soulspirit". One word. A tear fell down her cheek as a sense of coming home enveloped her.

Blake looked up at Henley for some explanation, but she just smiled and said nothing.

The butterfly flapped its wings, lifting itself into the air. The moonstone grew warm on Blake's chest with the closeness of her mom's memories. She could almost feel her there with them. Across the chamber the wall lit up with pearlescent light, illuminating the path into a previously obscure tunnel.

"I guess we go that way." Blake said.

Henley picked up her pack and buckled it on, gesturing for Blake to lead the way.

When they reached the path Blake realized that the lights embedded into the wall were moonstones, like hers.

A whisper of wind passed by them, carrying the words, *Blake Lucian, protector of dark and light. Welcome. We are waiting for you.*

Blake felt both betrayed and curious. Why did her mom keep this a secret from her? They could have shared the responsibility. Blake would have understood why her mom kept disappearing, instead of becoming angrier and angrier that she had prioritized work over her daughter. She was beginning to understand the gravity of her mother's work. It seemed that there was a spiritual balance between nature and mankind, one lost to the modern world. And now, she would have a hand in knowing its secrets.

The butterfly flew ahead of them. Blake stepped towards it, ignoring the mud under her boots, and pressed forward. They followed the pink creature down the tunnel and deeper into the cave.

After some time, they came to a fork. Blake crouched at the divide and pulled out some water. "Henley, what did my mother's note mean? When she said, 'I'm sorry I couldn't be the one.'"

Henley sighed and swirled her fingers in the dirt. "You know, the last time I was here was when your mom took her journey, not long after the last guardian died, when the moon waxed, like tonight." The butterfly landed on the infinity symbol Henley had drawn. "He hadn't finished teaching her all of the responsibilities of the role. It is often that way."

"So, was the last guardian a relative of mine?"

"No. He was not. It does not always pass down through one family. He didn't have any children, so he had to find someone else. His instincts led him to your mom. None of the guardians were surprised, your family has Lipan blood, the magic is within you. Your mom was a natural, serving as protector of the cave and keeper of the sacred."

"Why didn't Mirage save my mother? Doesn't it have that power?"

"No, my dear. Mirage doesn't work that way. When the cancer became too much for her, I took over her roles. That is why I moved closer."

Blake choked back some tears, thinking of the ignored calls still red in her phone. A reminder that her mom, and Henley, had tried to reach her multiple times. But Blake refused to pick up. She didn't want one more apology from her mom.

Before Blake could ask any more questions, a soft green glow crawled towards them from the left. The spider-like creature's eight legs carried its oversized body until it came to rest next to the butterfly. The butterfly kissed the spider with its antennae and flew back towards the entrance. Once again, a whisper filled the cave, *The weaver of fate steps towards you to guide your way.*

Blake put her hand out so that the spider could crawl into it. Luckily, she had never been afraid of bugs. The deeper they hiked, the more she felt that she already knew the way. She set the spider on her shoulder and leaned into her instincts.

After hiking for what felt like hours, time became abstract. The spider left a trail of glowing silk on the wall. Blake assumed (and hoped) it was to help them find their way back out.

When the tunnel opened to a rocky and narrow cliff, Blake pulled out the tether line and clasped her harness to Henley's. She couldn't see any permanent bolts in the wall, but thought being tethered together was better than nothing.

Their legs grew shaky as they descended step by step along the tight passageway, no end in sight. At times, small rocks slid out from under their feet, and they braced themselves on the cliff wall. They had no way of knowing how far they'd gone. As experienced spelunkers, they knew by the fact that their legs were tired, that they had covered miles of winding trails.

Blake caught another slippery spot but rebalanced. Henley wasn't so lucky. Her left foot slipped off the edge and the rest of her body began to follow. Blake braced herself, leaning back towards the wall, hoping to counter the weight of the body once it went over.

But instead, the spider leapt from her shoulder, fastening its silk web to the wall, around Henley, and back to the wall. The silk stopped her from falling over and was strong enough that she used it to lean on to push herself back up.

"Thanks little one." She pat the spider on the head and it leaned into the affection.

When they finally reached the bottom of the stairs, the moonstones stopped glowing. They must be a half mile underground now. Blake didn't know what to do. Her socks were wet. Her coat no longer kept her warm. And the lit path was gone.

It was in that moment that both of their headlamps went out. The dark enveloped them. Blake stopped and Henley bumped into her.

Henley reached for Blake's hand, gave it a squeeze, then sat down. "It's time, dear. You must go on. My journey stops here." The spider crawled into Henley's lap, curling into a ball like a kitten. Its glowing light not enough for Blake to see a path.

"But I don't know what to do."

"Yes, you do, sweet child, it is within you."

Blake closed her eyes, barely changing her ability to see. She took a deep breath, channeling her mom. She looked inside herself and began to let go. The cold seeped through her coat, but now it did not chill her. The darkness was all-consuming, but as she slowed her breath and focused on what she felt, she began to see with something else.

Henley's voice broke the silence. "We always get to choose. We get to choose to trust ourselves or not. We get to choose to use what is within us for good or for harm. If you accept this path, then you are believing in yourself and in your power to help this world."

As Blake breathed, she forgave her mother for not telling her about being a guardian. Another breath in and she embraced her own humanity, her weaknesses, and her fears. Understanding enveloped her. The good, the bad, the ugly, and the beautiful. It was in harnessing acceptance that she would be able to manage the ebbs and flows of life. Creativity and wastefulness. Compassion and cruelty. Experience and ignorance. Humanity and indifference. She made her choice to accept this role, whatever it be, and stepped into the darkness.

Blake felt the path ahead, as if being tugged by a strong river current. She allowed its pull, eyes closed, walking where the sensation led her. She felt the stone path descend underneath her, drawing her deeper. Eventually, it leveled out, turning left and then right, and back up again.

Blake's Soulspirit jumped within her. And then, without warning, the guiding sensation ceased. She opened her eyes. Darkness still. She could tell she was standing in a spacious room by the sounds the air made.

A small light began to glow, not too far away. She saw that the cavern was a perfect circle with no exits except the tunnel she came from. Even that was now closed, by a door like the one at the cave entrance. She looked around, trying to see what was causing her body to glow with familiarity, like when you see your dearest friend after missing them for years. The feeling of home, nostalgia, comfort, and warmth.

The voice whispered again. This time she saw that it came from the glowing orb at the center of the cave. It was Mirage, Blake knew this like she knew herself. Mirage was creation itself. The beginning, the light, the dark, the everything. Sitting around Mirage were her mother's friends. Napan Lupan, the Apache man, also known as Grey Wolf. Rowan Briec, a beautiful Celtic woman. Between them was the older woman, whom they had stayed with in India, near the Borra Caves. She was Veda Trivedi, knower of past, present, and future. There were others that she did not know. She sat beside Rowan. Henley appeared from thin air and sat next to her. They reached out their hands, completing the connection to make a circle.

She saw that the others had their eyes closed. She did the same. Mirage glowed within her, its energy pulsing in sync with Blake's Soulspirit, filling her mind with its history.

The truth of life is within you. You were born from it, and you will help to protect it. In the beginning we were all one. But the forces of nature are divisive. Humanity has the endless capacity to evolve. And yet, over and over again some of them choose to employ that power unethically. That is where the Guardians come in. You are now part of a long line of Guardians tasked with keeping the powers of creation hidden and safe from those who would abuse it.

We welcome you, Blake Alexandra Lucian, protector of dark and light. We see that your heart is true.

In the Night

Rochelle Sangabriel

It's still hours before the sun when Amelia's wailing wakes me. Intense and desperate, a sound so feral you want only to run away.

I vault from the bed and catch my toe on the boards that outline the mattress, set up as protection from The Hosts. I curse, waking Martha who pulls at my shirttails, but I shake her off and run out into the night, ignoring the crossbow that stands guard at the door, it's all but useless against them anyway and will only slow me down.

Without a weapon or benefit of a shining moon the night seems darker, more sinister even than before. With no shoes on my feet, I'm forced into a slow canter and the short distance to Amelia's cabin stretches out.

I don't know what drives me night after night. She only had the one boy and with him already gone the effort feels too much. But her cries are compelling, pregnant with anguish and despair. And I find myself always running toward them.

At Amelia's cabin I burst through the door, she no longer latches it.

'What right have you got not to latch your door?' I scolded, the first night. 'Do you know what that would do to your mother, to lose you too?'

'What else have I got to protect?' she asked.

She's on the floor now, her legs bent beneath her. The wailing has changed into more of a keening, still tortured but less urgent, so that at least I can hear my own thoughts.

I say her name once, then again at a shout, but she doesn't hear, or doesn't care.

I hastily search the room but it's always the same, no damage I can notice, not a thing out of place.

"Wally!" Amelia says. A pitiful, hopeless sort of sound. It brings me round to face her. Then she looks up at me, her eyes so empty, so red and swollen they're near closed up on themselves. Brings to mind the night it happened, a month past now.

———— ◆ ————

They'd come in the night and taken the baby without a sound or even the slightest rush of air. Amelia had known nothing of her child being gone until she'd awoken, and finding the crib empty, released that same keening, crying wail.

I'd run to Wally's cradle that night too. The boards were pushed to the side, splintered in places, pristine in others. The cradle was empty, as I'd known it would be, save an origami hawk: brown, black and midnight blue, small enough to fit in my closed fist.

I didn't know how it'd happened. Didn't really matter, they'd gotten Wally. There was nothing to do.

We erected a tiny cairn of stones in the back garden, next to Hank's grave. The ground's too hard for digging, least not til spring thaw. But Amelia screams each night. Calls out for Wally, rocks until there're bruises on her knees.

Martha bursts through the door now, only half inside her robe. The rest trails out behind her, a ghost at her back. She's aged ten years in the past month. She's done little but prepare stew and try to convince Amelia to eat. Amelia says she can't, the venison reminds her of The Hosts. She can't even stomach the curdled milk the children offer her when they come 'round.

I've kept myself distracted closing up the slivers of light that peeked through Amelia's water closet. I figure that's how they slipped in.

———— ◆ ————

I retrace my steps, back toward Wally's bed, hopeful of what I might find, scared too. But the cradle is empty and still. I circle the room, check the locks on the windows, try to stay busy while Martha whispers over Amelia. If I stay in motion, I don't have to admit the truth: They'll be back. Martha's moving Amelia now, she's helping her to the bed, easing her down and under the covers, stroking her shiny black hair and smoothing her nightgown. Singing her a lullaby that only sounds taunting and macabre now that the baby's gone.

What Hath God Wrought

Jillian Netherland

◆

Don't know where I come from or where I belong, but it sure as shit ain't here.

Name's Dally, short for Dallas, but that's only half of it. "Dilly-Dally", as I came to be known in my formative years, due to my chronic tardiness on account of having my head in the clouds, and the Dally part just stuck.

Don't let that fool you, though. I wasn't lacking intelligence or anything like that. I just knew, even as a kid, that I was neither for this world, nor was this world for me. Call it a coping mechanism or a self-preservation skill or whatever you like, but my brain was wired to help transport me somewhere else, anywhere else, making me the ever-distracted kid, the Dilly-Dally. Dally for short; Dallas if you please.

Now don't go thinking I had a bad upbringing that made me want to escape someplace else, because I didn't. Sure, I never knew who my dad was – still don't – and my mom abandoned me as an infant with a near stranger, leaving me with nothing but a name that was never hers to begin with and a broken down LaBaron. All of that's true, but so is the fact that Coop didn't have to step up and take in the baby of a woman he'd only crossed paths with the day before, but he did, and managed as good a job as anyone could expect from a man of his age and disposition.

That brief stretch of time Coop spent with my mom has been something of a myth for me, thanks to Coop not talking about it much. A head down, salt-of-the-earth type, Coop was born, raised, and lived his whole life here, with plans to take over his dad's garage after high school. That plan got delayed a bit, thanks to Nam, but true to his word, Coop returned from the war in one piece and started running the garage as if he'd always been doing it, which I suppose he had been, from the time he was able to pick up a wrench, anyway. So that's what Coop did, day in and day out, earning an honest living fixing cars and laying his head down at night in the little house on the same property, the very house where he'd done his own growing up, with very little change in routine.

That is, until Naomi showed up, passing through from one place to another with a conked-out car and a baby on her hip.

There are two things, and two things only that I know for sure about Naomi: one, Naomi ain't her real name, and two, she had some sort of a connection to Dallas, Texas. Coop and I pieced this together based on the two things she left behind when she disappeared: car keys attached to a keyring of the iconic Reunion Tower, and me, a son named Dallas.

It could be a coincidence, of course. Maybe she'd never stepped foot in the city and just had an affection for it based on something she'd seen or read. Maybe the keyring had been a gift and she just liked the sound of the name Dallas. I could spend my whole day speculating about the truth of Naomi, which believe me, I've done plenty of that over the years, and I've learned it always leads me back to the same place.

Nowhere.

Coop began that fateful day 28 years ago the same way he began every day: up before sunrise, two fried eggs, two slices of bacon, Texas toast with a generous slathering of butter, and a large thermos of black coffee before walking across the yard to the garage, ready for work by 6am sharp.

Despite being a small town with a meager population to match, Coop was never short for work to be done. Part of that was due to the townsfolk having a long history of trusting his family, knowing the price and the quality of the work would be equally palatable, and the other part was the location, right off the highway on a route known to be a preferred path for freight and travelers alike. While it wasn't common for people to move into our area *(or out of it, for that matter)*, it wasn't uncommon for passersby to find their way to Coop's garage in need of repairs or a tune up before heading on their way with a thank you and a smile, never to be seen nor heard from again.

Which is exactly what Naomi did.

It was that day, right before lunchtime, or so the story goes, that Naomi strolled up to the counter in Coop's garage with me in her arms, looking cool as the spring morning's breeze, despite walking 3 miles while carrying a baby.

The only two people who truly know for sure the details of their time together are Naomi, who I can't ask, and Coop, who won't disclose anything beyond necessity, so I only have a few bare bones facts to piece together the timeline.

Coop gave Naomi's car a tow back to the garage to diagnose the issue. Whatever it was needing done required a part he didn't have on hand and couldn't get delivered until the next day. I'll let your imagination fill in the blanks as to how the two of them ended up spending the night together at Coop's place, but I will tell you this: Coop was always a gentleman, so whether it was as simple as offering a single mom traveling solo a safe place to rest for the evening or something more, I guarantee he had every intention of cooking her eggs and bacon in the morning, but that was not to be. When he woke up, well before sunrise as was true to Coop's nature, she was long gone, while the car remained, and so did I.

It's not that Coop didn't try to find her. First thing that morning, the two of us took a trip to the police precinct.

"Coop! What brings you in?" asked the officer on duty, barely looking up from the coffee he was pouring. Nothing of concern ever happened around these parts, especially with Coop. The man minded his business to a fault.

"I'm looking for a woman," Coop began to explain. *"Petite, about 5'2, mid-20s I'd guess. Long dark hair, bright eyes, pretty face..."* he trailed off. Recalling details was difficult. He'd only known her a matter of hours, really. The officer found it hilarious.

"Ain't we all, Coop?" he laughed, clapping him on the back. It was

then that he realized Coop hadn't shown up alone and the officer's tone changed. The department put out a bulletin, seeking a woman matching Naomi's description, but unfortunately, Coop didn't get much information about her during their time together, and nothing was ever found.

Less than nothing, if we're honest. The plates on the LaBaron were bogus, registered to an elderly gentleman who had lived near Texarkana until he had passed, seven years earlier. Somewhat of a hermit, the man never had a daughter or a niece, or even an acquaintance matching Naomi's description, let alone any living relatives who may have known her. A dead end all around: literally and figuratively.

And so, that is how the timespan of less than a day, coupled with the decisions of one unknown woman derailed the course of both of our lives and at the age of 42, confirmed bachelor, Coop, married only to his routine, ended up raising a child on his own.

Coop never was much of a talker. Not in an unkind way, mind you. He was a man of few words but made sure every word he did say counted for something. Time was money in our line of work, and Coop ran the garage as a one-man show until I was old enough to learn the trade. Oftentimes, it would be tricky to hear each other between bays, so we'd communicate by tapping out Morse code on a stool, a tail pipe, whatever was nearest. Some nights we'd spend camping out in the yard, using flashlights to code messages back and forth on the nylon walls of the tent. His time in the military had imprinted this language into the very fabric of his being, and besides, we used fewer words this way.

"All meat, no filler," he used to say. Conversations were reserved for breaks and mealtimes; working hours were all business. I often wondered if he had held true to that value the day Naomi and I entered his life, but I was smart enough to never ask.

My status as the quiet kid with the funny name and just as much grease under my fingernails as in my hair didn't exactly earn me acceptance into the popular crowd in school. Being the daydreaming sort certainly didn't help. When I wasn't fixing cars with Coop, my nose was in a book, or my eyes were glued to a movie. Coop and I weren't struggling to make ends meet, but being the mechanic known for his fair prices didn't leave us with much in the way of disposable cash. Fortunately for me, Coop's place was just walking distance from the library where I could borrow books and movies to my heart's content, free of charge. Science-fiction, adventure, fantasy, whodunnits – I devoured them all. It was the closest I could get to leaving this world and joining a new one. Within these stories, I saw a version of myself where I could be anyone, do anything, exist anywhere. I could be the hero, the fighter, the lovable do-gooder everyone wanted to be near and celebrate – not that weird kid, Dilly-Dally, who smelled of machine oil and was left with a stranger by his own mother before his own story had the chance to begin.

As time went on and I grew into my teens, my appetite for escape could no longer be satisfied by books and movies alone. Attempting to fill the void, I began retreating into the world of drugs - psychedelics when I could get them - and the allure of a woman's *(and just one time, another man's)* bed. The town we lived in was too small, with everyone knowing everyone else, but once I was legally able to operate Naomi's old LaBaron *(my inheritance*, as Coop and I jokingly referred to it while we kept it running over the years), the world expanded for me, just a bit.

By that, I mean I could travel two towns over and become someone else for a few hours. Beggars can't be choosers, can we?

For better or worse, this new world of drugs and sex was introduced to me by my best friend, Jupiter. Jupe and I went all the way back to grade school, bonding over our goofy names. We were also both raised by just one parental figure with no known siblings to speak of, Jupe's mom as eccentric as Coop was grounded. As such, we were the outcasts, but while I internalized my feelings of not belonging, Jupiter embraced and weaponized hers.

"You and me, Dally. We're of a different origin. None of these skin sacks get it, but we do," she said to me one day during lunch in middle school. With a name like Jupiter, it's no surprise that her mom was one of those new-age hippie types, and the apple did not

fall far from the tree. As far back as I could remember, Jupiter would go off on tangents about the stars and energy that I still can't pretend to understand or care about, but I always admired her conviction in who she was, something I've never been able to achieve.

The first time I ever got high was with Jupiter. In fact, most of my coming-of-age firsts were with her, but you've got to trust me when I tell you there was never anything romantic between us. Sure, I'd be lying if I said I didn't find myself waking up in her bed from time to time after a good trip, bad trip, 6-pack of beer, or otherwise, but it wasn't like that. It's human nature to crave the comfort of another's touch, and with Jupe and me, well, we'd be hard pressed to find anything more comfortable than each other.

If you're thinking it's a sorry existence to spend my youth dreaming of something bigger, only to end up pushing 30 and in the same spot, drowning my discontent in superficial pleasures, well, you would be right. That's the dark side of small towns and routine. It's easy to become too comfortable.

Oh sure, I had excuses. I chalked it up to Coop needing my help at the garage (which was true, but he also continually made a point of reminding me that he fared just fine on his own before); or I'd tell myself I was saving cash to really make my grand adventures worthwhile when I got there (but instead, the money I made went directly into the pastimes that helped me escape temporarily, while simultaneously, kept me stuck in place). These self-imposed restrictions prevented me from pursuing all the dreams and desires I'd held close until I was slapped into a life-altering moment of seeing the light.

Coop died.

He wasn't my dad. He wasn't even my stepdad. We had no shared blood, nor adoption paperwork, but he was my family. Losing him brought all the emotions, questions, and longings that I had all but buried into perfect focus.

Life is too short. Plain and simple.

While I had spent the better part of a decade pissing away my time and money, Coop, unbeknownst to me, had been setting aside little by little at a time to leave me with a modest nest egg – including full ownership of the garage.

"What do I do with this?" I asked, plunking myself onto Jupiter's couch, probably older than we were, but comfortable all the same.

"I can't leave. It's his legacy, the most I've ever been given by anyone, but none of this feels - right."

"Oh, Dally," Jupiter sighed, cracking open a beer and handing it to me. *"Of course, you're on edge. The world you've known has been turned upside down, and on top of it all, you're right in the middle of your Saturn return."*

She said it so matter of fact, like these things were common knowledge that made any sort of sense to normal people, but I didn't interrupt her. Partly because I learned early on that there comes a time in a man's life where he has to pretend to not think astrology is a total sham if he values getting laid, but mostly because for all her quirks, Jupe's advice was always sound.

"Look," she said, placing her hands on her knees and taking a seat next to me. *"We've known each other, what, 23, 24 years?"*

I nodded. Truth be told, I couldn't remember a time when she hadn't been there.

"All you've ever talked about is getting someplace else, be it real or imaginary. The worlds you used to tell me about! For a while, I thought you'd grow up to become a writer or a movie director, or a slew of other things that would take you away."

I sipped my beer, staring at my work boots – a gift from Coop on my last birthday. Like everything around here, they were worn down, seemingly aging before their time. That's the bitch about time, isn't it? It passes before you've even realized it's begun.

"When we grew up and you stayed, I didn't push, because I was selfish and happy you were here. You're my best friend, Dally." She placed her hand on the spot between my chin and cheek, lightly turning my face so she could look me in my eyes.

"You're right; you don't belong here, and you do need to find more. Okay, so Coop named you owner of the garage, right? But being owner doesn't mean you have to be the one running it every day like he did, does it?"

And there it was, good old Jupiter wisdom.

It took most of the evening, a lot of brainstorming, and the remaining beers in Jupe's fridge, but together, we devised a job description, a budget to make the plan work, and a short list of people we could approach about filling the position - which ended up being much easier than anticipated. Turned out, Jupe's cousin had a buddy, Billy, fresh out of technician training. He had recently found his way after getting himself into and out of some trouble, so a clean start in a quiet town was exactly what he was needing.

—♦—

"Well, you did it -and here's to you," Jupe said as we toasted with our Miller High Life three weeks later. While neither of us were opposed to trying anything at least once, we were who we were, and fancy wasn't it. Celebrating with the champagne of beers it was.

Billy, or "The Kid" as he was better known, had just finished learning the ropes of running the garage, which, thanks to his training, didn't take much time at all. My responsibilities were fulfilled, and I had my savings from Coop, as well as my portion of whatever the garage would make after paying The Kid's salary to keep me afloat until I found my next source of income. I was free to go.

Arriving at the moment you've been waiting years to reach is surreal, to say the least. While you'd expect to be overcome by excitement, it's more than that. It's an incomprehensible mixture of joy, melancholy, anxiety, and anticipation all rolled into one heart-racing sensation.

"*So,*" Jupe began, playfully punching me on the shoulder, "*where to now, Mr. Grand Adventurer?*"

Wasn't that the million-dollar question? For all the hours, days, years, I had sunk into daydreaming, it was never one place specifically, but rather a galaxy of places, all calling my name. Still, when I thought about a starting point now, the answer was clear as day.

"*Dallas.*"

Despite never thinking it or speaking it aloud before, it came out so decidedly, like it had always been the answer within me, waiting for its chance to break free.

"I think, maybe, I can find some answers there. About me, or Naomi. If nothing else, at least I'll have had my adventure."

Jupe considered me for a moment, almost expressionless, before jumping up and nearly knocking me over with the intensity of her hug.

"Yes! Yes, yes, yes. Dally! This is exactly what you need to do!"

"You could go with me," I began. *"Lord knows you deserve a change of scenery, and we'd be great road trip buddies."*

Jupe let go, giving me a look I couldn't quite name, but had seen before. When we were kids, she found a turtle in the yard. We played with the damn thing all day, including it in all our tales of make believe, until the sun started to set, and we had to let it go back to the wild. I remember Jupe's face as she watched this turtle crawling towards the horizon. It was the same look she was giving me now.

"I can't do that, Dally. I've got my mom, and my clients – they need me."

Her clients, being the people who came around looking for weed, magic mushrooms, or a tarot card reading, sometimes all three.

"This is your journey, and I'll never be farther than a phone call away," she said, cupping my face with both hands. *"Find your truth, Dally. It will set you free."*

A couple days and a hefty security deposit on a one-room apartment later, and I was on the road in the old LaBaron. The trip in total only took about eight hours, making me kick myself for not taking it sooner.

No time for regret, though. First thing first – I needed to find a job. Rent in Dallas, even in a tiny shithole like the one I'd secured, far exceeded anything I had known - Coop's place had been paid off for ages, and this would be my first time paying rent anywhere.

I pulled over at the nearest gas station to grab a barbecue sandwich – shit, even the gas station food here was good – and began perusing job boards on my phone. Working in Coop's garage was my job history in its entirety, and while Dallas had no shortage of openings for auto mechanics, they all seemed to require this fancy certification or that one. Coop had taught me everything I needed to know; I had no formal training to speak of, at least not on paper. On to plan B.

I began searching for labor jobs: dishwashers, roofing crews, all in abundance, and then one caught my eye.

"Maintenance worker needed for overnight shift. Open interviews on site."

Coop had been a DIY guy and raised me the same, as the old house never had a shortage of practice projects. I was also a bit of a night owl anyway, so the overnight aspect didn't faze me one bit. The job was at an upscale hotel in the city and being unfamiliar with the area, I pulled up the address on the Dallas city map on Google. What I saw made my breath catch in my chest.

Next to the hotel was the same glowing structure depicted on the LaBaron's keyring: Reunion Tower.

———◆———

"So, you've had one job your whole life, no resume, and no references?"

It wasn't as much a question as it was disbelief. Abe, the hotel's General Manager, seemed enthusiastic to meet with me, but when I had nothing to show him beyond showing up, he seemed to find himself hovering somewhere between annoyed and perplexed. I wasn't out of the game yet, but I needed to choose my words with care if I wanted this conversation to go in my favor.

"That's correct, Sir. But I'm a hard worker, a fast learner, and I've yet to come across something I can't fix. If my previous boss were alive, he'd tell you the same."

Abe leaned back in his chair, rubbing his jaw.

"You mentioned you're new to the city. Whereabouts are you living?"

"The Southwestern edge of the city, Sir, just outside Oak Cliff."

Abe winced slightly. *"That can be a rough area. How's it treating you so far?"*

"I couldn't tell you, Sir." I began. *"I haven't been to my apartment yet. I got into town, grabbed a bite to eat, and came straight here."*

That got Abe's attention. *"You mean to tell me you drove all the way here and immediately began pounding the pavement?"*

"Yes, Sir."

Abe shook his head and chuckled. *"That's a strong work ethic. I like that. I'll tell you what, let's give this a try. Can you be here tomorrow night?"*

To say Naomi hadn't been much help through my life would be the understatement of the century, but in her own, uninvolved way, it seemed she had led me to landing a job.

———◆———

"Well, that didn't take long!" Jupe exclaimed over the phone that evening. I sat on the floor, cracking open a well-earned beer. I had made my way to a small, local grocery store to pick up necessities, but the one thing I didn't have was furniture. Not much fits in a LaBaron, and since I hadn't been sure how long I'd be staying, it seemed like a problem for another day when I had first decided to head to Dallas. I was quickly regretting this decision, as the long day was quickly coming to a close and I was desperately ready to catch some sleep.

"Can't say I'm surprised, though," I heard a long inhale and knew she was taking a hit off her bowl. *"You've always had this charm about you that people like."*

"You have definitely never said anything about my 'charm' before," I laughed. *"And besides, that ain't true. I don't know if you remember high school, but no one was getting pulled into the magnetic field of my charm."*

Jupe cackled. *"It is true, and I never told you because that head of yours doesn't need to get any bigger. But seriously, I'm happy for you, Dude! And right next to that wonky keyring tower! I always thought it kind of looked like an alien penis. Does it look like an alien penis in real life?"*

"Having never been up close and personal with an alien penis, I wouldn't know, Jupe," any question of what she was smoking now confirmed. *"But it is pretty wild that of all places I'd end up right there."*

"No," she said, a long exhale following. *"It's not wild. There are no coincidences, Dally. We may never know Naomi's reasoning behind anything, but she left you with that keyring, and now you're working right next to it. That's a sign."*

"A sign?" I asked, skeptically. *"A sign to do what?"*

"I've told you, Dally; this is your journey. You're the one to figure it out."

"Right," I said. *"On that helpful note, I'm going to hit the hay."*

"You mean hit the floor," Jupe giggled. *"Get some furniture, you bum."*

———◆———

I arrived early for my first shift, partially to impart upon Abe that he had made the right decision in hiring me, and partially because I didn't know what else to do with myself. Having a new city to explore and needing basic furniture took up most of the day, but when I'd had my fill of both, I found myself feeling anxious and ready to start. Running the shop with Coop had me accustomed to days that were both early and long; being awake at night wouldn't be challenging but adopting a reversed schedule could be a learning curve.

Abe wasn't in his office yet. No bother. I took the opportunity to people watch and absorb my surroundings, including the impeccable view of Reunion Tower.

What was Naomi's connection with this place anyway? I'd lie to myself and say I tried not to dwell on my mom, but my mind always circled back to her eventually. It must be a primitive thing that's etched into us at the soul level, to always wonder about our roots – not having those answers only amplifies it.

And then, the question that I always try to bury bubbled to the surface.

What kind of mother leaves her son and never looks back?

"Punctual, I see!" Abe's greeting snaps me back to the present, not a moment too soon.

"Let's get started, then. It's a big hotel and you'll need to know your way around."

Turns out the underlying focus of hotel maintenance isn't that far off from vehicle maintenance after all: fix what needs fixing, while preventing other problems before they reach problem status. After an in-depth tour of every seen and unseen corner of the hotel and meeting the who's who of each department, Abe presented me with a master key card and heavy-duty walkie talkie that looked like it had already survived World War III and could still endure the apocalypse.

"Quiet night so far, but that could change at any moment," he said, nodding towards my walkie. *"You'll find the preventative maintenance checklist on the desk in the manager's office with all the security screens. Make sure to log what you cover, but if any calls come through, those take priority."*

A quick handshake, and Abe was off, leaving me to make sure not just the biggest hotel, but only hotel I had ever stepped foot in continued to run smoothly throughout the evening. As of yet, my walkie hadn't proven to be anything more than a silent brick attached to my belt, so I consulted the maintenance list, each task organized into categories for efficiency.

Hotel exterior:
- Check for plants on building and foundation.
- Assess storm drain.
- Examine condition of walkways, portes-cocheres, & parking lot.

I wasn't accustomed to such big spaces with so many people inside of them, so getting outdoors sounded just perfect to me. Exiting the hotel's gigantic glass doors, I took a deep breath, feeling the heat of the day mix with the humidity of the evening along the exposed skin of my forearms. I can't say the inner-city air smelled fresh, nor were the sounds of Dallas nightlife peaceful by any means, but it was real, and more than that, it was new. I was here, and while I may not have been fully sure of what exactly it was that I was doing, I knew that I was doing it.

"Dallas?" a disembodied female voice echoed through my walkie. I fumbled with the belt clip. They can make cell phones thin as paper, yet nothing can be changed to make work walkies less cumbersome?

"Yes, Ma'am, what can I do for you?"

"Our guest in 305 has a clogged sink, and 923 had a lightbulb go out."

I smiled. Big city hotel maintenance was shaping up to not be so different from small town house repairs.

"Not a problem, Ma'am, I'll be right there."

Night one continued without issue and thanks to the checklist, the hours ticked by quickly and with purpose. I arrived back to my tiny apartment just as the morning sun began to peek through the blinds, happy to fall into a deep, fulfilled sleep on my new, less-than-comfortable-but-good-enough-for-now futon.

——◆——

Abe was already gone for the evening when I clocked in for my second night of work. I was pleased with the amount of trust and autonomy I was receiving already. Working with Coop all those years had instilled his work ethic upon me.

Keep chit chat to a minimum, but always be polite. Focus on getting the job done, and make sure it's one you can take pride in.

I strapped my walkie to my belt and headed to the manager's office to prepare my work plan for the evening. A note from Murph, the daytime maintenance manager, was waiting for me.

"Solid first night! You're going to make the rest of us look bad with your efficiency. Wondering if you could take a look at Elevator D in your downtime tonight? Complaints of the lights not syncing with the correct floor. I haven't witnessed it myself and want to determine if we need to bring in a tech or not. Thanks!"

I had barely finished reading when my walkie began vibrating, the scratch of static hitting my ears at full blast.

"Hello? This is Dallas in maintenance."

Nothing but garbled static. That was strange. I had no issues with the walkie's clarity the night before, but in a city as big as Dallas, the sheer volume of cell signals, airport towers, and GPS locators were bound to cause interference from time to time.

I left the office in search of a better connection. I had just turned a corner while rotating through channels on the walkie when I was interrupted by a rhythmic dinging.

Dah. Dit. Dit.
Dah. Dit. Dit.
Dah. Dit. Dit.

While focused on finding a clear signal for my walkie, I found myself directly in front of Elevator D. Whoever had reported the issue hadn't been kidding – something was definitely off. The floor lights at the top of the elevator kept blinking and dinging in a row, providing no indication where the elevator was in transit, but that wasn't what had my attention.

Dah. Dit. Dit.
Dah. Dit. Dit.

One long dash, two dots.
Morse code.

D.
D?
The Big D?
Dallas?
Me?
...no.
Could it?

"Dallas? Are you there?" The disembodied voice I now recognized as Tina, the night receptionist, transmitted crystal clear from my walkie.

"Hey, Tina," I unclipped my walkie. *"Sorry about that, minor technical issues. What can I help you with?"*

"Not sure if Murph connected with you before he left, but we've had some complaints about Elevator D going a little haywire – lights not syncing with the floors, doors not opening properly. Have you happened to notice anything?"

"Yeah," I cleared my throat, gazing upwards towards the lights, the rhythmic dinging continuing.

Dah. Dit. Dit.
Dah. Dit. Dit.
Dah. Dit. Dit.

"We're going to need to get that tech out here."

Night two proved to be as eventful as night one had been peaceful. Jupe's mom was an overnight nurse at our local hospital and often told us wild tales of the full moon affecting patients' behaviors. Moon talk in that house was nothing out of the ordinary, and I had always chalked it up as just that, talk - but the way calls were coming in left and right, from this guest's thermostat that wasn't working, to the lobby alarm malfunctioning, I could almost have bought into it.

Truth was, I didn't even know if it was a full moon or not. By the time I had a moment to catch my breath, the night sky was already fading to gold and it was time to head home. I was fast asleep almost as soon as my head hit the pillow, all thoughts of the elevator's cryptic dinging long gone from my mind.

I woke to the warmth of the midday haze peeking through the blinds to paint shadows across my face. I was never one to struggle with my own company, but something about waking to an almost empty room with bare walls seemed to emphasize how alone I was here.

I reached for my phone.

12:17pm, two notifications.

A bank statement email from the business account I'd set up to pay The Kid.

A text message from Jupe.

Hey, Night Watchman. Checking in. How's it going?

I smiled, the familiarity of my friend being just the medicine I needed to shake the morning blues.

Good start, work wise. Last night was a shit show, and these graveyard shifts are a bit of a bitch to get used to but can't complain.

Except you were totally just complaining :P

I rolled my eyes. Apparently geographic distance didn't matter; Jupe was still here to call me on my shit.

It's a beautiful wonderland of sunshine, lollipops, and rainbows. How's life back home?

I watched the three dots appear, disappear, and reappear, Jupiter no doubt crafting a witty, smartass reply.

That's the spirit! You know life here – not much to report.

Wasn't that the truth? I started to brew some coffee from the small, one cup coffee pot I had bought the day before, when my phone buzzed again.

It's weird without you, though. I miss you.

As in touch as Jupe was with her spiritual, emotional, and metaphysical self, she had never been one to get sentimental. This was new, but so was the two of us not being within walking distance from the other.

I miss you, too. You can always come visit, you know. We can tear up a new town!

The dots again, then a flower emoji.

I bloom where I am planted :)

Jupe's contentment in everything, always, was equal parts admirable and frustrating. While my constant internal state of restlessness was nothing short of exhausting, I could never understand how life in one place was enough for her. Thinking on it, a question rose to the surface inside me.

When I finally find whatever it is I'm chasing – will even that be enough?

The question plagued me the rest of the afternoon, mostly because I couldn't answer exactly what I was hoping to find here.

Who was Naomi?

Who am I, really?

Why did she leave?

Why have I never been able to satiate this tension inside of me, constantly threatening to burst through my chest?

My inability to assign purpose to this endeavor I had already jumped into headfirst – not to mention, the greater picture of my life as a whole, left a dark residue sticking to me, and by the time nightfall hit, I was more than ready to dig into my work for the evening, a warmly welcomed distraction.

"*Hello, Dallas,*" Tina greeted me with a friendly smile from the front desk.

"*Evening, Tina.*"

I dipped my hat and turned the corner, heading for the manager's office. I was feeling anything but convivial, but that was never an excuse to skip pleasantries and kindness, especially to those who have been good to you. Passing Elevator D, I noticed the doors had been plastered with caution tape, signifying the tech hadn't been able to make it in today. Sure enough, a note from Murph was waiting on the desk to tell me as much.

Hey Dallas,

Elevator tech won't be able to make it until the end of the week,. No issues with the doors that we've seen, but better safe than sorry. Make sure the caution tape stays up, and I'll keep you posted on the status.

Murph

Don't mess with the faulty elevator – simple enough. I began perusing my list for the evening when Tina's voice began reverberating from my walkie. I braced myself upon answering, hoping for a less eventful evening than the one before.

"Hey Tina, I'm here."

"Thanks, Dallas. I know it's not technically under your umbrella, but our Internet has been going in and out and Mark is gone for the evening. Any chance you can check the modem?"

Aside from upgrading our computer at the shop, Tina was right – this was not my wheelhouse. Still, what would it hurt to give it a look?

"Sure thing, Tina. I'm happy to help."

—◆—

I made my way to the commercial router in the telco room, unsure of what it was I was looking for, but didn't want Mark, the hotel's IT Manager, receiving an after hours call unless absolutely necessary. I switched my phone into cellular data mode and began Googling what to look for in a wonky modem, when it began power cycling on its own.

I'll reiterate - I am no IT expert, but I'm fairly certain that isn't supposed to happen.

I turned my focus back to Google as the modem rebooted, and then it started over again. I had reset our connection enough back at Coop's to know it takes a few minutes to complete. I began to amend my Google search for a third time, when the sound hit me.

Dah. Dah.
Dah. Dah. Dah.
Dah. Dah.

The modem continued its cycle, buzzing out the same repetitive pulse.
Dah. Dah.

Dah. Dah. Dah.
Dah. Dah.
Dah. Dah.
M.

Dah. Dah. Dah.
O.

Dah Dah.
M.

MOM.

I barely had time to process my mental translation of what I was hearing when my periphery caught the movement of someone darting out of the room. The figure had been dark, seemingly concealed in shadows, which puzzled me further. The telco room was small, about the size of a walk-in closet, not to mention, completely lit with overhead lighting– how had someone come and gone without my noticing?

Hello?

I exited the room, hastening my pace in pursuit of whomever had been hiding out. I was nearly to the lobby when I saw them, again in my periphery, rushing down a corridor perpendicular to my path. I changed direction to follow, but when I turned down the corridor, no one was there. This person was fast, and people don't run like that unless they have something to hide. I continued down the corridor, certain I would come upon them somewhere, when I was stopped by a rhythmic dinging.

Dah. Dit. Dit.
Dah. Dit. Dit.
Dah. Dit. Dit.

The trail had led me directly in front of Elevator D, chirping out its same message.

D.

Mom.

Jupe would say there are no coincidences in life. If that's true, then what was this?

———◆———

"Dally?" Jupe's voice croaked groggily through the receiver. I had just gotten home from my shift and my mind was racing too fast with too many thoughts to attempt sleep.

"Do you know what time it is? Are you coming off a bender?"

I wish this were a drunk dial. At least then I wouldn't care enough to question my sanity. I took a deep breath.

"I need your insight, Jupe."

I filled her in on what I had experienced the last two nights at work: the coded messages through the elevator and modem, the shadowy figure that had appeared and disappeared out of nowhere – and that I was beginning to think that someone, or something was trying to communicate with me.

"So, what do you think?"

Jupe let out a deep sigh that whistled.

"This is...a lot to process, Dally. It sounds like you've had an encounter with a shadow person."

"A shadow person?!" all efforts to stifle my laughter failed. *"How creative."*

"Shut up, Dally! This is serious. Look it up if you don't believe me. Plenty of people cite experiencing what you just described, more so these days than in decades past because heavy computer and screen usage has strengthened our peripheral vision. They appear dark because they are dark entities, Dally. Shadow people are not to be trusted. I'd get some sage if I were you."

Ignoring the sage comment, I considered the rest.

"Okay, I'll bite. Maybe this is some...supernatural shadow person,

like you say. It has to be connected to the messages though, right? Morse code isn't something everyone can recognize or pick up on – but I can. The coding D – on actual elevator D? Sure, I could write that off as anything, but then the modem spelling out Mom, when everything about Naomi has led me right here? Maybe she's trying to get through to me. Either way, I need to pursue this. Maybe tonight I can –"

"*DALLAS!*"

I shut up and straightened my posture. Jupe had never yelled at me like that before, nor could I remember her ever using my formal name.

"*I'm sorry,*" she began, clearly as shocked by her tone as I was. "*Listen. You've never had a mother figure in your life, and I am in no way volunteering myself to fill that role, but I have to step in when you're not thinking straight and could be putting yourself in danger. Truth be told, I don't know for sure what it is you're dealing with or what these messages mean, but what I do know is you have to be careful when you don't know what you're engaging with.*"

A long pause followed. Silence had never been uncomfortable between Jupe and me, but this one hung heavy.

"*Promise me you'll be careful, Dally. Don't let this void you feel suck you into something you don't understand.*"

I swallowed the lump in my throat I hadn't realized had been forming.

"*I promise, Jupe. You don't need to worry about me.*"

"*Good. I love you, Loser.*"

I laughed and shook my head.

"*Think you're going soft on me there, Jupe.*"

"*Shut up, Asshole.*"

"*Love ya too, Weirdo. And Jupe? Thanks.*"

"*Yeah, yeah. Any time, you know that. Clearly. Now get some sleep and let me do the same.*"

I took Jupe's advice. I got a solid eight hours of sleep and made a hearty breakfast when I woke: two eggs, two thick slices of bacon, and a Texas toast, the Coop special. I made it a point to drink water and get outside during daylight to boost my endorphins and make sure I was in a place to start work that evening with a clear head. By the time my shift rolled around, I was feeling good, ready to focus on the night's work ahead.

I made my way towards the hotel's revolving glass doors, the last of the day's sunlight sinking into the horizon behind me. As the doors rotated, I caught Reunion Tower's reflection in the glass, the pillar that had started it all, yet I still hadn't visited. Tomorrow would be my first day off since starting the new job – the first full day to myself in my new city, perfect timing to check it out.

"Evening, Tina, " I said, greeting her with a smile this time, determined to make this night better than the last. Mind over matter was another virtue Coop had drilled into me over the years, and I resolved to put it into practice.

I made room for myself at the manager's desk, setting down my thermos of coffee, and looking for any notes from Murph. When there wasn't one, I took it as no news was good news and began to review the maintenance checklist to see where we left off.

Buzz.
Spark.
Flash.

Being as small as it was, and not planning to spend much time sitting before getting to work, I had left the office door open, allowing a view of the hallway from where I was sitting.

Buzz.
Spark.
Flash.

One of the wall sconces in the highway was flickering. This could be something as simple as changing the light bulb, or it could be indicative of a more complex, electrical issue. Hoping for the former, but bracing myself for the latter, I got to my feet to examine the light fixture.

Buzzsparkflash.

Buzz. Spark. Flash.
Buzzsparkflash.

I took a step backward, rubbed my eyes, opened them again, and stood frozen.

Buzzsparkflash. Three quick flashes. S.
Buzz. Spark. Flash. Three long flashes. O.
Buzzsparkflash. Three quick flashes again. S.

S. O. S.

Jupe's warnings echoed in my mind as I reminded myself that everything I was perceiving went against all logic.

I also knew that S.O.S. was a distress signal. Someone was calling for help, and to ignore it would be worse than irresponsible, it would be negligent. The question wasn't whether I would help, but how could I help, when I had no idea who was asking for help or from where?

My mind raced, remembering the ways Coop and I had communicated through Morse code over the years: car parts, work benches, headlights. I turned my attention back to the manager's office, on the hunt for anything I could use to tap out a message, settling on a flashlight.

Taking a breath, unsure what to expect, I pointed the flashlight towards the sconce.

Two quick flashes.
I.
One quick flash and one long flash.
A.
Two long flashes.
M.
Four quick flashes.
H.
One quick flash.

E.

One quick, one long, and another quick flash.

R.

One quick flash.

E.

I am here.

I repeated the pattern twice more. Nothing. I stared at the sconce for what felt like an eternity before laughing and shaking my head. My shift had barely begun and here I was, willing a light fixture to communicate with me. Maybe these night shifts were taking more of a toll on me than I had anticipated.

Buzz. Spark. Flash. Buzzsparkflash. Buzzsparkflash.

The sconce sparked to life, repeating a familiar code from the last few days.

One long flash followed by two quick flashes. D. This time, it continued, increasing in speed each time.

Buzz.Spark.Flash.Buzzsparkflash.Buzzsparkflash.

Silence. The sconce continued to flash, but its buzzing sound – and all ambient noise from the hotel – dissipated at once, as the corridor went completely dark, sans the light from the sconce flashing D over and over. My skin prickled as the hairs on the back of my neck stood at attention in response to the breeze passing over my body, despite being nowhere near a window.

And then it was over. I stood in a warmly lit, climate-controlled hallway lined with high-end sconces, all functioning properly.

A loud, rushing sound approached me and I spun on my heels, preparing to be charged. In the corner of my eye, I caught a shadow darting down the corridor to my left. Responding more to reflex than thought, I chased after it. Unlike last time, the shadow stayed with me, shifting between my left and right periphery.

It wants me to follow, I thought. Not knowing if this was a good thing or bad, curiosity won over logic and I continued my pursuit, my breath quickening in my chest and sweat beading on my forehead and under my arms. I pushed through until I could no longer see the shadow and the trail went cold.

Stopping to catch my breath, my head down and hands on my knees, I heard a familiar dinging in a new pattern. Looking up, I saw the shadow had led me directly to Elevator D.

Dit. Dah. Dah.

Dit. Dit. Dit. Dit.

Dit. Dah.

Dah.

Dit. Dit. Dit. Dit.

Dit. Dah.

Dah.

Dit. Dit. Dit. Dit.

Dah. Dah. Dit.

Dah. Dah. Dah.

Dah. Dit. Dit.

Dit. Dah. Dah.

Dit. Dah. Dit.

Dah. Dah. Dah.

Dit. Dit. Dah.

Dah. Dah. Dit.

Dit. Dit. Dit. Dit.

Dah.

What hath God wrought? The first official Morse code message ever transmitted – but what did that have to do with, well, anything? Puzzled, I stared at the elevator's lights as it repeated its ambiguous message through dings, when shadows began darkening my periphery in both eyes at once, closing into a tunnel.

"Dally," I heard a voice say as arms wrapped around my torso, pulling me backwards. I spun, the shadowed figure fully in front of

me for the first time. The figure continued to pull me into its arms, the cold I'd felt previously in the corridor now enveloping me.

"No," I pushed the figure, the hairs along my arms continuing to rise as a field of goose flesh took their place along my skin.

"Dally," the voice repeated, the figure now in front of me, its long fingers weaving their way around my wrists.

"Get the fuck off me!"

I shoved the figure just as Elevator D echoed one final ding, its doors opening wide. The figure tumbled down its shaft, but not before clutching my forearms and taking me down with it, the shadows closing in again as darkness swallowed me whole.

They tell me Jupe died on impact. Our phone conversation had left her with an uneasy feeling of needing to check in on me herself, so she finally decided to take the trip out of town. Her goal, I'm sure, was to save me from whatever she feared I was chasing. She ended up saving my life by breaking my fall with her own body.

I've tried to reconcile that night in my mind over and over, but no matter how many times I revisit it, it's never Jupe's face I see, or any face at all. Just shadows, and that voice I should have recognized anywhere but didn't. My thoughts, once consumed with questions about Naomi, now replaced with questions for Jupe.

How confused she must have been with the cruelty in which I spoke to her.

The thoughts that ran through her head as she fell to her death - the fall I caused by pushing her.

How betrayed she must have felt if she had time to feel or think about anything.

I can't pretend to know what happens to us after we die – Jupe would have been the one to have some theory about that. I hope somehow, she knows how sorry I am, that if I'd only known what I was doing, it never would have happened.

I hope she knows I loved her, and that I still do.

I hope she knows I'd do anything to go back to that night and trade places with her.

Before I left town, Jupe told me the truth would set me free; that's not always true. Turns out, the court of law frowns upon vague messages from inanimate objects leading to dysfunctional senses, even if it is the truth.

Abe, Murph, and Tina were all brought in for questioning. I wasn't there. My public defender tells me they all had the same comments: they knew me only briefly, I was hardworking and seemed like a nice guy, they were shocked. Some folks from home wrote letters, saying how they knew me my whole life, the Dally they knew was no murderer, especially not to the person who had been attached at my hip until I came to Dallas. It didn't matter. Jupe and I were found at the bottom of the elevator, my injured, but intact and breathing body on top of hers, completely crushed and devoid of life. The hotel cameras also caught our entire exchange on video, showing just the two of us outside the elevator together, where I unmistakably pushed her to her death.

Jupe's mom also wrote me a letter directly, filled with questions I can't answer.

My unwavering conviction in the turn of events deemed me unfit to stand trial, landing me a one-way ticket for an all-inclusive stay in this starch white hospital with its constant glaring overhead lights.

With the two people who ever cared about me in the world gone, I don't get visitors. What I do get is endless time to think, mostly about them. Coop was not my dad, nor was Jupe my girl, but maybe what I had with them was something better. We had no family obligation or titles holding us together. We were family because one day, we chose to be, and we continued to make that same choice every day until the very end.

And isn't that the irony of it all? I spent my entire life wishing for something more and now I spend every minute of every day wishing I could go back. All the years of discontent and restlessness now feels like such a waste when everything I could have ever wanted was everything I already had.

I lay on my bed. The godawful fluorescent lights buzz above me.

Nothing.

The old pipes rattle.

Nothing.

Call me crazy – the state of Texas does – but I find myself wishing and looking for coded patterns, just for some sort of conversational company. Real or not real, it doesn't matter anymore. Not much does.

I still don't know where I come from, or where I belong, but it sure as shit ain't here.

Pastries & Potions

Tara Henderson

$\blacklozenge$

Miriam keeps herself busy in her charming café, which is barely a blip to the passersby. She hums to herself as she sprinkles her favorite herbs into some lattes. Many Dallas/Fort Worth airport travelers with frequent flyer miles to rival that of pilots walk past countless times before the scent draws them into *Stars Aligned: Coffee, Spirits, and Tonics*. The wafts of cinnamon, baked apple, and lavender snap them from their zombie-like saunter towards gate A23 or C27.

Outside her café, oversized art pieces reinforce the stereotype that everything is bigger in Texas. New arrivals can be made to feel insignificant next to the large windows and ceilings, expansive like the wide-open spaces of the Texas Plains. The ones who have time before their flight find themselves compelled to turn in for a snack. The cafe is always packed.

"Hey Jenny, can you please take this to table twelve." Miriam hands the waitress a tray filled with cookies and lattes.

"Sure thing, boss."

Miriam stands behind the bar. The emerald tile backsplash and marble countertop greet the clients with a clean boho chic vibe. They feel like they have entered another world, distinct from the cavernous walkways packed with noisy restaurants and crowded shops. That is because every morning when Miriam arrives to the café, she conjures serenity with a simple wave of her hand.

Like a doctor reading the symptoms of their patients, Miriam watches the travelers, analyzing their words and their body language. Everyone benefits from her simple concoctions, like the hungover college students that Jenny just delivered the turmeric lattes too. But she especially likes to watch for the ones with a weakness that needs healing. The airport serves as her undercover base. A café – the ideal conduit for her to brew enlightenment, truth, and dreams fulfilled.

Her gift for magic arrived, like most witches, at the age of twelve. Her mother knew the signs, having been the daughter in a long line of magical women. Until her 18th birthday, when her mother dropped her off at the Coven, Miriam spent her weekends learning the history and knowledge of her people. Like her ancestors, she wanted to use her magic for good, not speak theoretically all day at headquarters in a hidden house at the edge of a secret road in the middle of a thick forest.

The Coven was helpful, for a time. In their kitchen she combined her love of ancestral baking with their knowledge of the elements. Using various combinations of ingredients, she crafted recipes to cure headaches, increase motivation, or provide protection from danger. She would stand tall, wipe her hands on her apron, and smile as they praised her work.

As she looks out at her customers, she feels the same pride. So many lives have been helped from her potions. Travelers relaxed a bit more, people had new ideas, and even relationships were mended.

Back at the Coven, as time passed, being under the witches' thumbs became stifling. They limited her freedom in the kitchen, kept ingredients locked away, and reprimanded her for making potions outside of class time. Staying there was crushing her creativity, like Michelangelo's would have been had he ever been forced to paint a stick figure!

She had to escape. The training had served its purpose. So, five years ago she left The Coven and began putting the techniques into real world uses. What was the point of harnessing the old ways if they weren't going to share the benefits?

Here, at Stars Aligned, she has complete freedom. Lattés and muffins serve as vessels for balance or intellect, depending on her customer's needs. She sees clues to their needs in the sideways glances to the person they are with, or the sigh they heave after hitting send on an email. One time she watched an exhausted young mother juggling three children by herself on the verge of tears. She gave her Werpoes, which strengthens the body. Miriam returns to work each morning anticipating the opportunities to deliver her magic culinary delicacies.

Today, a couple sits at the bar, barely speaking to each other. The woman wears an engagement ring. Both of them are staring at their phones and both look about as happy as a patient awaiting a colonoscopy. Miriam's fingers begin to tingle, her magic prodding her to act. Maybe they just need a little nudge, to urge them to be honest. Yes, that will be perfect. Miscommunication is, after all, one of the leading causes of breakups. People constantly sabotage their own well-being. She smiles as she sprinkles Elysian into the man's Mocha Latté. Let him be the vulnerable one.

Miriam wipes her hands on her apron and walks away to attend to some tables. She carries a warm brownie to table nine and collects dishes from table seven. She is surprised when, not ten minutes later, she sees the fiancé grab her bag and exit through the security doors. The ring sits on the counter in front of the gentleman. His latté gone.

"I had to tell her the truth," he mumbles. It's more to himself than to Miriam. "I don't want to marry her."

'Flight 478 to Cancun, now boarding.' The PA system announces.

The man checks his phone, shrugs his shoulders, leaves cash on the counter, and heads across the walkway to board his flight. Miriam adds the ring to her cookie jar in the shape of Saturn, which sits on a shelf behind her.

Another interesting outcome. Not the one she was expecting, but avoiding years of an unhappy marriage is a success by any account. Honesty is always the best policy. Her mother loved that saying. She cleans off the counter and heads to the next customer at the bar.

"I will have a pink Chai muffin, please," the older woman requests.

"Excellent choice." Miriam turns to warm it up. All the muffins have Cedronian, an ingredient that promotes balance. Everyone benefits from this.

She returns to the woman with a warmed muffin on a plate. "What a lovely café you have." She takes a bite of the muffin. "Oh, the Cedronian is barely detectable."

Miriam startles, then looks at the woman more closely, now recognizing her as Agnes, the assistant to the Coven leader. Miriam turns to run, hoping she can find a new place to hide, away from the inexorable crones. But her feet stick to the ground. Unable to move, she looks back at the witch.

"We've been looking for you for some time now." She takes another bite of her muffin. "Clever strategy to set up at an airport. Pinpointing where the disturbances came from was tricky."

"Disturbances?"

"Miriam, you can't use magic on humans without their consent." The witch waves her hand, turning off the lights and flipping the sign to 'closed'. Customers did not seem surprised by it. They gather their things and leave, all of them with a blank expression on their face. Miriam senses it. Agnes must have buzzed the air, causing a stupor to fall over her clients.

Agnes continues, "There have been far-reaching consequences from your unsolicited doses of Elysian, Galifrazian, and Night Blooming. Reports of inconsistent behavior, exceptional leaps in skill, and inexplicable relationship developments finally led us to you. The only thing that all your victims had in common was a recent flight through the DFW airport."

"Victims?" Miriam is abruptly silenced, and her feet start moving towards the exit, neither of her own accord. Agnes is smirking, thinking that she's one step ahead.

Jenny comes from the side, opens her palm, and blows just the right amount of hemlock powder into Agnes's face. Jenny catches Agnes as she starts to fall, setting her body behind the counter, where no one will be able to find her. She will wake up tomorrow and feel as if she had the best night's sleep of her life. No harm done.

"Well, boss. I guess it's time to go."

With Agnes passed out, Miriam is freed from her spell.

The two women take a minute to pack up Miriam's extensive collection of herbs, plus the Saturn cookie jar, and then they head to the parking lot. Miriam moved cities four times in the last five years. When she met Jenny in Portland three moves ago, she made her an apprentice. Jenny was a fast learner, just like Miriam had been.

Miriam looks back at *Stars Aligned* and allows herself a moment of sadness. The airport had been a great base, their longest location so far. The café will soon belong to someone else, and she will have to find a new way to help others. Magic is not meant to be reserved only for the few who can harness it. Her fingers tingle yet again, sensing the next perfect location.

The Seven Devils

K.I. Runyon

◆

Today was the 18th of May 2023 and so far this year, Mari had thought about ending her life no less than one-hundred and thirty-six times. She'd had a good day last Tuesday where she forgot to think about it for more than a minute so she didn't count that day.

Also, about a month ago, they took a family trip to the beach over spring break and she'd lost her phone. She hadn't spoken to anyone for a whole day before her mother had gifted her a new one. That was a good day too. Two out of one-hundred and thirty-eight days.

Today, though, the feelings were suffocating her. As she dressed for the ceremony in her room, a prototypical messy teen room, she looked in the mirror. Mari didn't appear sad or depressed. In fact, she'd perfected the vision that reflected back at her.

Her long blonde hair was styled into beach waves. Her soft brown eyes framed in mascara didn't look teary or bloodshot. She turned around to get a better look at the back of the lace white dress that covered her chest, extended to her elbows, and reached her knees. How could anyone fault her?

Mari's hands became clammy and her vision spun. It was getting harder and harder to pretend that it was all *fine*. She couldn't tell anyone how she felt, of course. They wouldn't understand. What could Mari possibly be upset about?

Her parents loved her. Her brother was nice to her. Her boyfriend doted on her. She wasn't unpopular. She didn't have to diet like her friends on the cheer squad because she had a naturally fast metabolism and she was already five foot seven. Even school didn't require half the amount of effort as people complained it did. It was just memorizing facts for fucks sake.

On top of that, they lived in gods damned Highland Park. People would sell their soul to live in this exclusive suburb of Dallas. And here Mari was trying on her third Chanel dress, wondering if this would be the one she'd wear to watch her brother graduate. But it was too hard to decide with Barb frowning at her.

Oh yes, Barbara. How to explain. That was where it had all gone to shit. Mari was seeing people. People who shouldn't be there. And very specifically, seven people. Well, six, but more details on that later. At first, Mari had googled bipolar disorder. Apparently that wasn't it. She didn't become these people. They were simply there, taunting her every moment of every day.

She wondered if maybe she was schizophrenic but she didn't quite agree with that diagnosis either. Mari functioned normally and was able to ignore them for the most part. It was simply annoying to have them sitting there watching her every move and judging her actions. They were like ghosts but with a little color and a lot of attitude.

Currently, Barbara, the most vocal of the Seven Devils, as Mari nicknamed them, tsked at her as she pulled her heels on.

"Don't you think you should have worn the second one? That one was at least covering your ass," Barbara said as Mari started to leave her room. Mari sighed. There was literally nothing wrong with the length of her dress.

Barbara, or 'Barb', looked like a forty-year-old soccer mom. She had short, brown hair and wore khaki pants with various color polo shirts. Barb trailed behind Mari and complained every time she wore a skirt that wasn't at least two inches past the point where her fingertips ended against her thigh.

When Mari inevitably ignored Barb, she whispered words at Mari like "slut" and "whore" when she left the house. The good news was that Barb got tired after a few minutes and usually disappeared before Mari made it to her destination. It was very similar to her mother's nagging. Mari reached the bottom of the stairs where said mother stood.

"Are you finally ready?" she asked. Rainey Sutherland was an older version of Mari. Her blonde hair was in a fancy French up-do and she wore a dark blue wrap dress with six-inch white heels. Gorgeous, if one had to describe her.

Mari didn't miss the annoyance in her mother's tone as she aggressively tapped on her phone, no doubt giving one of her underlings some new command to follow while she was out of pocket. Mari's mother was a high-powered attorney who somehow managed to kick ass and never miss a single moment of her children's lives, even when they didn't want her there.

"Honey, are you ready? Your mother's impatient to get good seats," her father, Henry, said, joining them in the foyer. He was a decent father. Nice, though somewhat absent, and thought the entire world revolved around his wife. He had that all-American look that all the girls swooned over. Also, blonde. It made Mari want to gag when she heard their old college stories of how they met.

Henry Sutherland did exactly whatever his wife told him to at all times. He might be CFO at Renfrow Oil & Gas Co, but he was a lowly servant in his own household and he loved it. And now he was making excuses for her mother's rude behavior as he always did.

"Yeah, let's get this over with," Mari said, walking toward the garage.

"We are not 'getting this over with' Mari. This is a very important day for your brother. It's not every day one graduates from high school with an early acceptance to Stanford and a full ride to play football. Be a little self-aware, dear. It's unbecoming," her mother lectured as they got in the car. Mari did everything she could not to roll her eyes.

Her older brother, James, the aforementioned graduate, was a varsity wrestler, football player, and track star. How he managed to do all those things at once Mari didn't know. Especially since he fucked anything that breathed, including men and women. He was up front about who he was at least.

As Mari slid in the backseat of her father's Escalade, Mariana appeared. Mariana was a fickle Devil. She only came by a few times a week. She was no more than five and looked weirdly a bit like Mari had when she was little, following her around asking 'why'.

Mariana wore a pleated blue dress with a starched collar and her long blonde hair was pulled back in a big white bow. Mariana questioned every move Mari made. Good or bad. Go to a movie with James. *Why?* Stay home and watch a TV show. *Why?* Go to a party. *Why?* Read a book. *Why?* Mariana kept Mari on edge.

"Why?" Mariana asked, as they pulled away from the house. Mari, per usual, had no idea what Mariana was alluding to. Mari ignored her companion on the way to the ceremony, hoping she'd be gone by the time they were seated. It was hard to ignore the Devils in public. Mari couldn't keep up with all the conversations at once and Dale would be appearing any minute now.

When they arrived at the stadium, which, because, once again, Highland Park was reminiscent of a professional football arena, Mari's mother led them straight to the front row of the parents' section, where someone had saved them seats.

Mari barely suppressed a groan. Her mother had arranged their seats and still had the nerve to rush them? Mari wanted to scream but she dutifully sat down and smiled at people as they passed by.

"Oh look, there's Lia," her father said, unaware of Mari's inner turmoil. Mari looked across the seats to see her squad mate Lia. Lia waved furiously, her brown ponytail bouncing, eager to show the other people in this hell hole that she knew the Sutherland family. Mari gave her a half-smile and a short wave.

Looking at them sitting there in the front row, the onlookers could only assume that Mari had the perfect life, just like her brother. Mari was captain of the cheerleading squad even though she was only a junior and had a perfect GPA. She also had the boyfriend everyone was jealous of, Benjamin.

Benjamin Harris Worthington, the third, as he was legally known, was James' best friend. He was over six feet tall with dark brown hair and blue eyes. The kind of guy anyone would drool over. He'd never cheated or tried to play games with her like others his age and he always called Mari to ask if he could go hang with the guys even though her brother teased him mercilessly over it.

Despite all this, there was something inherently wrong with Mari's life, even before the Incident. She'd always been different from her family, not quite as cheerful and as enthusiastic about their privileged life but after that night, she knew that there was a cost associated with this life. There was a toll to pay if you wanted to live it and she didn't know if she wanted to. In fact, she desperately did not want to.

The Seven Devils were getting worse. Besides Barbara and Mariana, there was also Dale. Dale was a dick and he was the most relentless. He usually spent most of the day with Mari. He was a chain smoker in his fifties with a beer belly, wore a wife beater, and leered at Mari all day.

Every time she gave Benjamin a kiss or a hug, Dale would chuckle like he was getting ready for his favorite show. When Dale had showed up a few months ago, she stopped being so affectionate with Benjamin. It helped but it hadn't made Dale leave. Benjamin noticed, but as always, hadn't pushed her. She wished he would.

The next Devil, and her favorite if she had to choose, was Kristy. Kristy was a fuckin' trip. She was the only one who wasn't completely out to get Mari. Mari thought of Kristy as more of a frenemy. She'd shown up about a month after the Incident and sounded a lot like her former best friend, Renee.

Renee used to be someone that Mari could be somewhat honest with. A person who'd get Mari out of her weird funks, but ever since Renee had failed to stop the Incident, Mari couldn't trust her so she'd been slowly but surely pulling away. Renee didn't notice or at least, like Benjamin, didn't push Mari on it. Mari wondered if any of these people actually gave a shit about her. You would push if you cared, right?

Kristy said the same things that Renee used to say but with more bite. During cheer practice, "Really? Does Desiree honestly think that jump is going to keep her on varsity? I could do that in my sleep. Not you, though. You've been slipping lately too." And Kristy was right. Mari's jumps and cheers were good, technically, but there wasn't any passion in them like there had been before.

In class or after school when she was doing her homework, Judy showed up. She looked a little like Mari's grandma before she'd died but angrier, meaner. Judy carried around a flask, wore the same dirty purple sweater each time, and used a walker.

Judy would whisper into Mari's ear while she was thinking about how to tackle a problem, how dumb Mari was, or how her grades were going down so she shouldn't bother to try anymore. Mari pushed through but Judy was right. Last week Mari had gotten a 'B' on her history test. Her mother had reamed her for over an hour. Judy sat there sipping on her whiskey smiling maniacally during the whole thing.

Mari had googled cliffs in Dallas before she'd gone to bed that night. Unfortunately there weren't many in the area where she could drive her car off or she'd used the wrong search terms. She settled for jogging on her mom's treadmill until she'd collapsed into a heap of exhaustion. She'd find a solution to this all soon enough.

Then there was Ben. He was essentially a bad boy version of Benjamin. He looked the same but dressed in leather jackets and ripped jeans. He also had a scar that ran the length of his cheek. Not unlike the mark she'd left on him that night.

Ben constantly said things that made Mari sad. She was a bad girlfriend. She was a liar. She cheated on Benjamin and would break his heart if only he knew. Any time she was with Benjamin, Ben was there too, taunting her. She needed to break up with Benjamin soon. Ben had been pushing her to do it ever since he'd appeared. Mari wasn't good enough for Benjamin. She shouldn't hold him back.

Mari was only waiting for Benjamin to leave for college. Once he did that, she would encourage him to go play the field at NYU. He didn't need to wait on her. Besides, she wasn't stupid. She knew how great Benjamin was, and smart too. He could do better than some broken brat from Texas.

Mari's mother nudged her, bringing her attention back to the ceremony that was about to start. Mari squirmed in her chair, so uncomfortable that she could barely breathe. She didn't want to be here. In this crowd. In this place.

As soon as it started then he would be front and center. The final Devil. Except he was very real. He was the one who starred in her nightmares every night. He, unlike the others, was definitely not a manifestation.

The blood on her legs, the scratches she'd inflicted on him, the bruise around her neck from when he'd held her down. Those were real. No matter how hard it became to stay tuned to reality when the rest of the Devils were circling her, she knew it had happened. Remembered every second of it.

Principal Deerfield, a mouse of a man with a stick up his ass, came to the podium and tapped on the microphone to get started. The crowd quieted down as he introduced himself and welcomed the seniors. One by one they filed in. The actual Devil lead the way. As quarterback and valedictorian, he was the first to enter. James and Benjamin weren't far behind.

Mari saw black spots dot her vision. She couldn't do this. She couldn't watch them all celebrate this monster. His fake smile and the charming glint in his eyes dazzled the crowd. She tried to get up, to leave. Her mother grabbed her arm.

"This isn't the time Mari. Please. We're celebrating James now," she scolded. Mari sat back down. Felt her body tune out, the same way it had done before, after the Incident was over. She felt the eyes of the other Devils form.

"Whore," Barbara whispered from behind. Mari's toes curled as she watched the smoke from Dale's cigarette go up into the air.

"Honestly, I mean, you're like way hotter than his girlfriend but she is a better dresser. I don't know why he chose you," Kristy said. She sat on the step next to Mari, out in the aisle of the stadium, wearing the high school's cheer uniform.

"Why?" Mariana asked. Mari closed her eyes and breathed deep, the voice of the worst Devil coming through as he welcomed friends and family to the ceremony. She wanted to throw up. But then suddenly, the voice stopped, and the next speaker came up.

Mari opened her eyes, saw Benjamin looking for her. She waved and he smiled brightly. She smiled back. A fake one, but better than the one she'd given Lia earlier. Benjamin's joy calmed Mari down enough that she regained her ability to breathe.

The rest of the speeches passed in a blur and Mari thought of several new ways to end this farce once and for all while she waited for Principal Deerfield to declare it over. Mari even let Judy sneer at her some more while her mother berated her yet again for losing focus earlier.

Later in the day, after a fancy celebration lunch for James, she went to Benjamin's house for his own graduation party. Mari tried not to cringe while Bad Boy Ben harped on her for having the nerve to attend. She and Benjamin would be breaking up soon after all. Mari kept going through the motions.

Mari even nodded along and pasted on a fake smile when Renee showed up and told a funny story about how she and the Devil were going to do long distance. Renee's parents were friends with Benjamin's parents so Renee had to come to Benjamin's party first, then she'd go to his. Mari's palms were dripping with sweat by the time Renee was gone.

"Everything okay Mari?" Benjamin asked when she left later that night. His eyes were slightly glazed from the couple of beers he drank and he wore the NYU baseball hat he'd bought on his tour earlier this year.

"Of course," she said, even though she screamed, *help me,* inside. But she couldn't yell loud enough over Ben telling her to end things.

"You can tell me if something's wrong. You know that right? I love you. We can figure it out together. And even if..." He took a deep, shuddering breath. "Even if it's not me that can help you or that you want, I'll still support you." He squeezed her hand. She leaned in on her tiptoes and kissed him on the cheek.

"I love you too," she said, meaning it and wanting it so badly to be enough. "Don't worry. I'm just thinking about next year and how it'll suck. That's all." The lie sat like rotten eggs at the back of her throat the whole way home but he bought it. Better he never knew what she was really thinking.

The next day while her parents were at church – remember, perfect, Texas, God, Country, all that – she rummaged through their medicine cabinet. She couldn't do this anymore. Dale and Barb were getting so fucking loud. And Ben. He wouldn't stop. Even Mariana was getting more annoying. They were destroying her.

Mari read the labels carefully, looking for a drug she recognized. Ibuprofen, Zofran. Not quite right. Xanax. That could work. She Googled it. How many to take to overdose, but it wasn't easy to figure out. Could you overdose on Xanax? She didn't know. It looked more like there would only be damage, not death. Finally, she hit the jackpot. Sleeping pills.

She opened the container and found it was almost full. There must really be a god out there because he'd finally given her a sense of hope. Peace was near. She slipped the container in her sweater pocket and put the rest of her mother's things back in place the best she could manage. She would take these tonight before she got into bed. Only another ten hours or so until the Devils would go away forever.

That evening, she sat at the desk in her room contemplating whether or not she should leave a note and what she would say when the doorbell rang. She quickly put a draft version of said note under a book and peaked out of her door and down the hall. Her brother was also upstairs and did the same. He wore a Stanford sweatshirt and basketball shorts, his hair sticking up in different directions, and had a game controller in his hand.

"Are you expecting someone?" he asked. She shook her head 'no' and then grabbed a baggy black sweater to put over the tank top she was wearing to go down. No need to provoke Barb unnecessarily.

She and James went down the stairs together, but her parents beat them to it. They'd obviously opened the door and she could hear voices. Official sounding voices. "Sounds like the cops," James said, clearly confused. Mari's heartbeat picked up.

"Mari," her father called and Mari froze, half-way down the steps. "Can you please come down?" James stopped and looked over at her. Someone knew. No. Her parents couldn't know. Benjamin couldn't know. He'd never look at her the same. Mari's eyes widened in panic.

"Mari, come on," James said, his voice gentle. Maybe because he was her brother, or maybe because deep down under all that golden boy bullshit he was actually a good person and he sensed that she was seconds away from running, he took her hand gently. "One step at a time, Mari." She followed him numbly.

There was a woman in plain clothes with a badge in her hand and another male officer in uniform with her. Her parents stood next to each other in the foyer, both with looks of concern on their faces. The female, a detective maybe, saw Mari, saw the way James was leading her down. In that moment Mari saw it. The detective's eyes softened. She knew. The Incident was no longer a secret.

"Mari, honey. These officers want to ask you some questions about Renee's boyfriend, Michael. There's been a situation, apparently," her father said. Mari flinched at Michael's name and her whole family stiffened at that reaction. How dare her father say the Devil's name out loud without warning.

"Maybe we could have a seat," her mother said. For the first time in Mari's life, her mother sounded uncertain. More like a mother, less like an attorney. James led Mari over to the couch in the front sitting room and they all sat around each other. James never let go. The female officer leaned forward.

"Mari, there's no easy way to say this, but Michael Sutton was caught sexually assaulting a sophomore at a party last night. His girlfriend, a Renee Briggs, walked in on it. She called the police and we brought him into the station. We can't tell you who the girl was because of her age and privacy concerns but she, uh," the officer cleared her throat and looked at Mari's parents before returning to Mari.

"She said that it wasn't the first time. And that, he told her that she was a stand-in. A stand-in for you, Mari." The words sunk in around the room and Mari felt the tension seeping into the air. Mari's jury of Devils sat and watched, waiting to see how she'd react.

Mari let the feeling of hopelessness settle over her. Benjamin would know that she was unclean. Her parents would need to deal with their problem child, maybe send her to a different school. Only James didn't give away any indication of how he was feeling.

"Mari," the officer said, penetrating the eerie quiet of the room. Mari could vaguely see the outline of tears welling up in her mother's eyes but she couldn't acknowledge them. Mariana was asking why again. "Did Michael Sutton ever hurt you?"

Mari looked over at Dale. She swore she could smell the cigarette smoke despite knowing he wasn't real. He leered at her. Who the fuck was Dale supposed to be? Everyone else was based off of someone she vaguely knew but Dale. He was a wildcard.

James turned her toward him and put his hands on her face. He looked deep into her already misting eyes and then he spoke. "Mari. If he put his hands on you, please tell them. Do not let him get away with it. Do this for you. Not for me, not for Renee, not for this officer. Not for anyone else. Did he hurt you?"

Mari nodded once up and down. James' hands tightened around her face slightly but then he swallowed thickly and wrapped an arm around her shoulders. Mari fell into his familiar frame using him as a shield.

"When did this happen?" the detective asked, scribbling on a notepad she'd pulled out at some point.

"Almost seven months ago," Mari said, her words low and quiet, barely above a whisper. A Devil had appeared for every month that had passed since the Incident, including the original one.

"They," Mari gestured, still unable to look at her parents, "took my brother to a college tour out of town and I went to a party. Renee got sick and I went looking for her when she didn't come back. I found Michael in a bathroom cleaning up. He'd put Renee to bed. And then he," she stopped. Ben was screaming at her.

"You asked for it, you whore," he said. She looked at him, in the corner of the room.

Mariana was asking "why?" while Barb echoed Ben's words. They were all out, all of the imaginary Devils that had started harassing her the day the true Devil ruined her.

"Honestly, you went to the party," Kristy said, her biting words at odds with the casual way she was leaning against the wall filing her nails.

"Shut up," Mari cried, finally speaking directly to one of the Devils for the first time. Her parents, the detective and the officer, and James all paused and looked over at the corner of the room.

"Is...ehem, are you talking to someone sweetie?" her dad asked, the first to recover.

"They never stop," she whispered, covering her ears with her hands. The detective took over, telling her parents about post traumatic stress disorder. They stopped asking questions. They tried to put Mari to bed, but they found the pills and the note. They rushed to the hospital. Mari spent four days there and when she left they went straight to the police station.

When Mari walked out of the station, having given her full statement, and felt the sun shining on her face, there had only been one Devil left. The one who'd desperately tried and failed to destroy her. He still stole her dreams and most of her nights but the days were now blissfully quiet.

It took longer for the rest of the world to return to normal, but what the fuck was normal these days anyway? For Mari, it was the fact that today was August 24th, 2023, and she hadn't contemplated suicide for seven whole days.

Magical Transgressions

Amanda Kennedy

—————◆—————

The dawn hours were Kendra's favorite for indulging in the forbidden pleasures of Magic.

Lying in bed with the soft sounds of her three younger sisters' breathing all around her, she reached her hands out and pulled the stale air from the room and ushered it under her bedclothes. She felt the blanket rise from her warm body, allowing cool air to sweep in. Gooseflesh prickled beneath her nightgown. The blanket floated higher and higher, hovering all but one corner that still grazed the edge of the mattress. Her fingers burned hot with the effort. Almost! She watched the corner lift a little more...

"Breakfast, Kendra! Time to get up."

Her mother swung the bedroom door open, startling Kendra. In a flash of motion, she let the blanket drop, then flung it off, and sprung from the bed. "Yes, Ma! Be right there." Her words came out fast and high pitched, but she couldn't help it. Shame quickly replaced the delight she'd held only moments before. All the heat from her fingertips receded.

The door closed with a soft, unspoken accusation. Kendra put her hands to her face and groaned into them. Even if her mother hadn't seen, Kendra knew that her face and voice likely gave her away. Accepting that nothing could be done about it now, she pulled her nightgown up over her head and grabbed her work robes from the hook above her bed. After dressing quickly, she busied herself with making the bed extra neat and tidying her share of the room to perfection, as though an extra measure of goodness might lessen her wickedness. She left her sleeping sisters and reluctantly walked down the hall towards the warm kitchen.

At the wood stove, Kendra's mother was bent over, pulling hot biscuits from the belly of the oven. "Good morning, Ma!" she said with forced cheer. There was no response and Kendra wondered if this was a silent punishment for practicing Magic or if her mother was especially focused on her task. Regardless, she thought it best to put some space between them as soon as possible. Her stomach growled at the smell of fresh biscuits, and she grabbed an apple from the table. Her leather boots stood by the front door, and she made her way over to slip them on.

"I think I'll take breakfast with me today. I want to get an early start on the wall."

"Suit yourself," her mother answered. "Here," she took two biscuits from the baking sheet and slid them across the worn wooden table. "Take these with you."

Kendra grabbed the steaming biscuits, her seventeen-year-old fingers just as tough and calloused as her mother's forty-year-old ones and reached for the door latch. It was clear that neither of them wished to acknowledge what might or might not have been going on in Kendra's bedroom that morning.

"Bye!" Kendra pulled the door closed before she could hear her mother not say goodbye in return.

Her spirits lifted as soon as she stepped out of the oppressive air of the kitchen. Not for the first time she wondered if her mother or father ever practiced a little harmless Magic themselves when no one was watching. Surely, she wasn't the only one guilty of this transgression.

The pink and gold sunrise cast an ethereal light over the land. She paused to take in the picturesque landscape that was all hers in these early hours. One of the few perks of being called as the bricklayer. That, and the privacy it afforded her. Her father had been the sole bricklayer for The Order until his back injury three months ago. When it was clear that he would not improve enough to allow him to return to long days of physical labor, Kendra was called upon to replace him. She had been expecting it, just not this soon.

At first, she'd felt a heavy resignation to the calling. It was hard work and generally regarded as low status. Since completing her schooling this year, Kendra's classmates had been assigned callings ranging from Officiator of Ceremonies to City Assembler. While the latter was merely maintaining roads and public spaces, it was still held in more esteem than bricklayer.

When she was a child, helping Pa at the wall had been fun. Being the oldest of seven children meant that quality time with either one of her parents was rare, so it was a special treat to have his attention all day. She avoided chores with her siblings, earned extra portions at meals, and enjoyed quality time with her father.

She'd missed the company of others during those first few days. Which was a surprise to her given that she had no close friends. She was lonely at first, but it wasn't long before Kendra grew accustomed to the work and discovered that being left alone had its advantages.

She departed from the main road and walked east towards the rising sun. Dew covered the grass, and she left boot prints in her wake. It was only a short walk up the hill to the brick wall that encircled The Order. It had been erected generations ago after the first wizard introduced discipline to the elemental Magic held by Kendra's people. In Kendra's own family, earth and air Magic ran strong from both her parents and each of Kendra's siblings held the ability to manipulate either one. Except for one of the twins who took after a great grandfather on her mother's side and possessed power over fire.

Protecting her people's Magic from those who might wish to exploit it for their own gain was necessary to their peaceful way of life. And, while the Elders preserved the sanctity of Magic in The Order, the rest of the members fulfilled callings to contribute in their own way. The firstborns in Kendra's family had been called to be bricklayers for as far back as her family knew.

The wall was impressive. Easily standing twice the height of Kendra, it encircled their land and had taken her ancestors decades to complete. Maintaining it was Kendra's full-time job now. The section she was working on today was an older portion of wall showing the signs of sagging that come with age.

But, before she started her work, Kendra looked forward to treating herself to a little private Magic practice.

Everyone knew that Magic was only sanctioned for use within religious gatherings by those in authority. According to history, Magic had been passed down from generation to generation since the first wizard was bestowed with the sacred gift. Now, only Elders, the appointed ones who made up The Order, openly practiced in the bordered land within the wall. Kendra's people thrived under the protection of The Order, and Magic practiced within sacred ceremonies honored its history. To preserve the sanctity of Magic, it was important that it not be used carelessly. Imagine how Magic would be cheapened if every housewife was using it to hasten her water to boil in the name of cooking potatoes faster. The idea, all agreed, was blasphemous.

Still, it didn't stop some from practicing in small, discrete ways. Apart from the ultra-pious, most turned a blind eye to subtle Magic used harmlessly. Like, when starting the morning fires, no one commented when flames leapt up after minimal effort over the hearth.

Once, Kendra had even witnessed an elder open a fissure in the earth to drop a piece of chewing bark into. He'd closed it up neatly with a swish of his fingers and scuffed his foot over the crack beneath his robes.

These were the things she told herself to justify practicing Magic in the early morning hours before starting her work each day.

Last week Kendra taught herself to pull water up through the earth into a small crater she'd opened. Obviously, a new lake wouldn't go unnoticed by folks, but if it began as a puddle, and she was patient enough to grow it slowly, she could make a decent pond for her younger siblings to play in by next summer. Today she would focus on pushing the depth a little more while leaving the width alone for now.

In fact, as she approached the wall, she could see the orange reflection of the rising sun in her small pond. It brought a smile to her face, and she quickened her steps. In her excitement to reach the pond, Kendra didn't notice at first that her brick cart, which she'd left full yesterday, was mostly empty and the portion of wall she'd been repairing was completed. When she did see it, she stopped in her dewy tracks as though the earth held her in place.

"What?" she asked to the empty meadow. She cast her eyes all around, shading them against the rising sun, then forced her feet to come unglued and step forward, closing the gap between her and the wall. As she got closer, she looked for clues. Her cart, stacked high yesterday, now held only a few dozen bricks. Next to it was the bucket in which she mixed her mortar, looking rinsed and cleaned. Her tools, once belonging to her father, were cleaner than she'd ever seen and neatly laid out on the cart.

Kendra crept forward and ran her hand over all her things, as though they might transfer by silent osmosis some answers as to what had happened in her absence. Receiving no messages from the inanimate objects, she went over to inspect the wall. The work, she grudgingly noted, was immaculate. The bricks were level and true, the mortar's granular texture smooth and flush to the surface. Whoever had done this even managed to stagger the bricks in relation to the existing wall around it, creating visual continuity as her eyes swept left to right, and right to left. It was better, she admitted to herself, than even her own careful work.

A splash from the little pond interrupted her inspection of the wall. Reflexively, her fingertips burned at the ready with Magic. The surface of the water was disturbed but there was nothing else amiss that she could see.

"Who's there?" she demanded in a voice much braver than she felt. "Come out!"

Kendra went over to the pond and knelt to peer into the clear water.

"Is that a...?" she reached a hand into the cold water and pulled out her answer. "A rock?"

Laughter came from behind the wall.

"Who are you?!" she demanded. "Show yourself now!"

An amused voice called, "Got your attention, didn't I?"

She waited, flexing her fingertips.

A pair of hands appeared over the top of the wall and pulled up the body they belonged to. A mop of light brown hair emerged, and a young man hopped to the ground just as easily as he had pulled himself over the high wall. He stood before her looking pleased with himself.

Kendra spoke first, eager to possess the upper hand in this unexpected situation. She would not show fear to the outsider. "Was this you?" She pointed to the wall behind him. "Did you finish my wall?"

The man's appearance was disheveled in an attractive boyish way that Kendra was doing her best not to acknowledge. His smug smirk should have annoyed her, but only added to his good looks. Kendra hoped her own glare was intimidating.

She tried another tactic. With arms tensed at her sides, and fingers splayed out, she pulled the air from around her and forced it upon her target. Unprepared for the blast of wind, he stumbled on his feet for a moment but quickly regained his nonchalant stance. He looked delighted by her blasphemous show of Magic, and he clapped his hands, which only vexed her further.

"Oh, Kendra! That was magnificent!" he said. "But watch this." He directed her attention to the ground between them with his bright eyes.

Despite herself, she looked down and saw the grass trembling. Then, to her disbelief, thousands of dewdrops clinging to the blades of grass began to let go one by one and lift into the air. Kendra was transfixed by the sight of innumerable water droplets trembling to hold their shape as they levitated higher and higher. The sunrise, still painting the sky in brilliant pinks and golds, was reflected in the water droplets and created an illusion of tiny sparkling gems, floating in the air. They rose ever higher, pulling her eyes upwards to the sky. She watched, dumb with wonder as they stopped rising and hung in place, suspended. It was as though time had been frozen. Kendra reached out a fascinated finger to touch one, which released a small deluge of pink and gold rain onto her face and robes.

"Hey!" She jumped out of the way too late, which incited ecstatic laughter from the stranger. Now she really was mad. "Who are you and what do you want?!" She spat the words at him, finding it much easier to be enraged with a face full of water.

"Yes, let's do this properly, shall we?" He swept his arm between them in an exaggerated show of manners and said, "Let me introduce myself first. I'm Leff."

"Ok, Leff," she tried hard to not be disarmed by his charming, easy nature. "You already know my name, so with pleasantries out of the way, why don't you tell me what you're doing here."

"Same thing as you, Kendra." His eyes twinkled. "Magic."

For the second time this morning, gooseflesh broke out over her arms, and it wasn't from her cold, wet robes. She'd heard of people like this who held no regard for the sacredness of Magic. People who flaunted and perverted Magic for their own needs and pleasure. These people were swiftly exiled from The Order.

However, if she was honest with herself, she had removed Magic from its pedestal long ago. She may be more like Leff than she would like to admit, but at least she had the decency to make a show of respect, she thought. Never had she heard someone openly talk about using Magic. His cockiness was brash.

In a small voice Kendra tried to bring some decorum to this irreverent exchange. "Practicing Magic outside of the sanctity of The Order is a violation of nature." She knew it by heart as one of the twelve tenets of The Order she memorized as a young child in her studies.

Leff rolled his eyes and took a step closer. "You don't really believe that do you?"

"Hey! Don't come any closer. Actually, why don't you leave? I have work to do." Her eyes flicked over to the newly repaired wall, which made Leff grin.

"Doing what?" he asked. "Fixing this wall? Why? You've been told it's to keep you safe from people like me. But it's to keep you in. To better control you." He lowered his voice and took a step closer. "Kendra, I've watched you out here and seen the joy your Magic brings you.

"Is this -" He bent down and picked up a small twig. A flame sprung up from one end like a candle. He passed it to her the way a child might present a plucked flower to their mother. Kendra accepted it, appreciating the beauty in the dancing flame. "- unnatural?" he finished.

"What do you want?" she repeated, looking into the flame as she spoke.

"I want what you want. To be free to practice Magic in all the ways that bring me joy. I want to share it with others. I want to find meaning in my Magic and not have it dictated to me by a group of people hoarding all of its power for themselves. I want to free others from the oppression of The Order, and I want someone to help me do it. I want to dismantle it brick- "he took a small step closer, "-by brick."

Kendra continued to stare into the flame as he spoke. She felt the heat of the flame from the stick, but more than that she felt the heat of magic in her fingertips. And it did not feel wrong.

"I can't," she managed, finally tearing her eyes from the glow of the flame. When she looked up, she was startled to see him standing so close, but she didn't step away. Leff kept her gaze, not saying anything, and she felt compelled to go on. "I have a job to do for my community. For my father." She looked back to the fire she still held, and a decision seemed to flash across her face. She blew the flame out and tossed the stick to the ground. "I can't," she repeated, this time with more conviction.

If Leff was disappointed it didn't register on his face. His smile only widened, and he quietly asked, "Kendra, does The Order make you happy?"

It was a simple question, delivered with kindness, but Kendra bristled, crossing her arms over her chest and took a big step backwards. "I am happy!"

Leff laughed, all at once offending and charming her. "Oh, and you look it, too!" He put up his hands in mock defense.

"Look," she went on. "You don't know me. You don't know anything about my life here." As the words came out, she wondered how true they were. He already knew her name and had obviously been watching her practice Magic for some time now. She shook the thought away. "Why do you care if I'm happy anyways? If you're so happy with all your free and irreverent use of Magic, then what are you doing over here on my side of the wall?" She was emboldened by this notion; this proof that his way of life had perhaps led him to seek out the purpose and order on her side of the wall. She took a step closer, closing the gap and attempting to gain the upper hand once more. "What are you looking for, Leff?"

She didn't understand what happened next. Not at first. A soft breeze, impossible in the still morning air, caressed her cheek like an invisible hand. Kendra whipped her head around, although she knew they were alone. The same soft breeze, warm like her breath, brushed her hair back from her face, then moved to her backside, pressing her towards Leff. Her mouth opened in surprise, and a soft "oh" slipped out. Their faces were now inches apart and, still, he hadn't answered her question. Or had he?

Kendra's heart pounded in her chest, and she felt heat everywhere, but not from the Magic within her. Her eyes met his and locked. Leff dropped his eyes to her lips, and she lowered hers to his. They moved in closer, the kiss all but done until Kendra halted.

"Wait."

This time, Leff's face did betray his disappointment. He quickly recovered, running a hand through his messy hair. "What?" he asked.

The look on Kendra's face was that of someone solving a complicated riddle. Her brows drew together, and she looked at her brick wall as though seeing it for the first time. The last several minutes played back in her mind.

"You-" she began, words and thoughts tripping out, not fully formed. "The rock, then water from the grass..." Her eyes darted around as she put it together. "You lit the stick, too. And the ..." she recalled the air's touch on her skin but couldn't say the words. Finally, she brought her eyes back to his. "You possess all four elements," she said, incredulous. "Like me."

Leff nodded, "Like you."

Anytime Kendra allowed herself to acknowledge that she possessed power over all four elements, it was alongside the knowledge that people like that existed only in folklore. Fantastical, old tales woven to entertain children at bedtime. In the realm of giants and trolls. So, while she enjoyed her magical gifts privately, it was a lonely secret to bear. She finally understood why Leff was here.

"We're the same," she whispered.

"Yes," he said.

Kendra was the first to smile. Small at first, then, encouraged by Leff's easy grin, uninhibited and full of joy. She was not alone! Here was someone else who knew both the burden and the delight of being capable of shifting the earth beneath your feet, manipulating water's flow, harnessing the wind, and calling on fire from within. What a relief it was to be seen and understood for the first time in her life.

If Leff's identical expression meant anything, then he felt the same.

"Let me show you, Kendra," he said, softly. "Step outside these walls and see for yourself. Make up your own mind."

Kendra barely flinched when he reached out to take her hand. What did surprise her was how natural it felt to hold this boy's hand mere minutes after meeting him. The heat from his own fingertips lit the fire in hers. Leff's gaze shifted slowly from Kendra's eyes to the brick wall, and they turned away from one other, still holding hands, to face the wall.

At first, it was just a low hum that vibrated the ground beneath their feet. It grew in sound and intensity until the blades of grass trembled and Kendra felt a low rumble in her chest. She squeezed Leff's hand, and he squeezed back. Small cracks from the ground up began to appear on the wall, like slow-motion upside-down lightning. The cracks widened until pieces of the wall began to break off and fall to the ground, littering the grass with mortar and brick.

If she felt any objection to the destruction occurring in front of her it was overshadowed by the magnificence of it. Although Leff had initiated the demolition, Kendra effortlessly, and without thought, joined him. With her free hand, she made a fist and rotated her wrist one way, then the other. Soundlessly, and without flair, the ground beneath them began to soften, squishing beneath their boots as ground water was pulled to the surface.

The first piece of wall to give in to the wet earth was no wider than a door and the wet grass accepted it with a dull thud, spraying

Kendra and Leff with drops of water and mud. They laughed and jumped out of the way. Never had Kendra felt so alive. What a release it was to express herself so freely. Like she'd been holding her breath all these years and she had just now been allowed to fully take a breath.

More pieces of the wall fell; some falling towards them and some falling into the thick woods, which was now fully visible beyond the broken section of wall. The trees and tall grass were thick, though Kendra could see a narrow, trampled path that someone had worn down with repeated visits to the border.

Leff, she assumed.

Kendra turned to look back at her community below her. The Order. It was a tidy representation of the safe life and belief system she had grown up with. Small cottages spaced evenly along straight and narrow roads. Most chimneys gave up smoke from morning cooking. The smell was familiar and comfortable. A few robed figures could be seen walking, most likely heading to their work callings or to a neighbor's house. Beyond the houses, public buildings nestled among trees, shrubbery, and green spaces. And encircling all of it was the wall.

Kendra's wall. It contained her family, her history, her people, and her beliefs. It contained her childhood, her memories and, previously thought, her future. She turned back to the crumbled pile of bricks before her. She did not want to be contained anymore.

Releasing Leff's hand, she reached both palms behind her, fingers splayed wide. The leaves in the trees shook and the surface of the water in Kendra's little pond rippled. A breeze, pulled from the still air behind her, was ushered forward and billowed hers and Leff's robes. Their hair blew wild and crazy around their faces. She brought her hands forward and the rocks and rubble littering the ground began to roll, barely at first and then as though pushed by invisible hands. Chunks of brick and mortar swept left and right, clearing a path through the center of the hole in the wall. The last to go was the dust and small debris, smoothing a clear trail that lined up with Leff's worn trail into the woods.

Leff's mouth hung open. "You," he began, searching for his next word, "are amazing, Kendra. Wow."

This was by far the most brazen act of magic she had ever attempted, and she was thrilled that someone was here to witness it. Someone who was as awed by her gifts as she was. It was amazing, she thought. She was amazing, she admitted to herself. She took Leff's hand again.

"Ok," she said, agreeing to step through the wall. To see and make up her own mind. His smile reached all the way up to his eyes, crinkling them at the corners.

"Shall we," he asked, nodding to the forest. She nodded in reply and together they walked forward. They stepped through the wide opening, an entrance into an exciting new adventure for Kendra. The sun, now lifted well above the horizon, did not reach inside the forest. The dark, shaded woods gave Kendra pause. She had never been in the woods; never been beyond the wall.

Uncertainty replaced her courage and she faltered next to Leff. Feeling her stalled beside him, Leff stopped and turned to her, then looked to the woods where she was staring with a thin frown on her face. Quickly, he scanned the ground at their feet. Kendra looked as well, curious as to what he was searching for. His face lit up when he spotted something in the tall grass and released her hand to reach for it.

He picked up a stick, about as large as his arm and held it firmly in his two hands. Kendra watched as first smoke, then a blackened tip grew at the end. It didn't take more than a few seconds before it glowed red, then burst into a beautiful flame. He held it out to Kendra, and, like the first time with the twig, she was mesmerized by both the beauty of the fire and the tenderness in the gift.

She reached out to take it and felt the heat on her face. The glow of the flame illuminated the smile on her face. Leff's gift would be just enough light and comfort to guide her way forward.

He extended an open palm towards the path, an exaggerated gesture of chivalry. "After you."

Editor's Note

The Kindred Writing Collective was born when two friends became writing accountability partners. With Writing Down the Bones (Goldberg, 1986) as their guide, Amanda and Tara dedicated one to two hours a week to reading a chapter and then writing from the prompts in the book. When they reached the chapter, "Writing is a Communal Act," Natalie Goldberg said:

It's good to know some local people who are writing and with whom you can get together with for mutual support. I tell my students to get to know each other, to share their work with other people. Kill the idea of the lone, suffering artist.

The idea to join a writing group was born. After searching for local in-person writing groups and coming up empty handed, they realized it would be up to them to make a group.

Tara, an experienced event coordinator, and Amanda, a connoisseur of books on writing, were a perfect team. They reached out to the Coppell Cozby Library and pitched their idea. On January 2, 2020, their first meeting was held. Ten people showed up. Amanda and Tara were amazed.

From 2020 to July 2021, they continued this journey with the library. As their writing progressed, it became clear that if they were going to take themselves seriously as writers, they would need to become an exclusive group, no longer accepting new members. The members who were showing up consistently were invited to meet at Tara's house and anyone who was ready to take their writing to the next level chose to become part of this new, exclusive group.

By shifting away from hosting new writers at each meeting, the

Kindred Writing Collective was able to create a safe space for its writers to challenge themselves, hold each other accountable, and watch the magic of intimate friendships unfold.

With the encouragement of each other the writers started monthly author spotlights, submitted pieces to writing contests, and shared their goals with one another. In the trusted circle they began to distinguish themselves as the editor, the cheerleader, the spiritual guide, the tough love, the articulate question-asker, and the beta-readers. All of them embracing the role of being the first fans of each other's work.

Like most journeys the Kindred Writing Collective took on a life of its own. While each member continued to lay claim to their preferred genres, short stories became a perfect vehicle to branch out into different or unfamiliar genres. Within a short story, the romance writer can attempt fantasy, and the memoirist may try her hand at horror.

It was through years of prompts, exercises and curiosity that the group generated a number of pieces worthy of sharing.

Wanting to create a pathway to publication, the idea of an anthology was born. The Coppell Cozby Library hosts an annual Indie Author Fair, and with that as their deadline, the first edition of the Kindred Writing Collective Anthology became a reality. Within its pages are the evidence of hours of learning, sharing, editing, and growing. The human journey is varied and vast, full of chaos and uncertainty. But when we take the time to nurture relationships, especially with a common goal in mind, beautiful possibilities emerge. It is in that spirit that we write. We write for each other. We write because it brings us joy. And we write for you. Our readers. We hope you enjoy the first edition of the Kindred Writing Collective Anthology.

About the Authors

IZZY THORPE

Izzy Thorpe is a serial hobbyist. She enjoys painting, drawing, gardening, reading, and, of course, writing. That and curling up on the couch with her cat and a hot cup of tea. Izzy writes to share her perspective on the world and to share the wild stories that float through her head.

TARA HENDERSON

Tara never could have predicted that volunteering to be Amanda's writing accountability buddy would lead to her becoming an author! Her writing journey started in the second grade when she got a pink diary with lock and key for her eighth birthday. Journaling is where she started again in 2018 with Amanda. But by the end of 2022 that writing practice developed into a writing group, a novel, two NaNoWriMo wins, a blog, and a workbook published on Amazon. With her passions for building community and encouraging intentional living, Tara continues to write workbooks and publish content @honestly_Tara on Instagram. She lives in the suburbs of Dallas, TX with her husband, three teenagers, a dog, a cat, and a Google calendar that rivals any CEO. She loves the Kindred Writing Collective and the people in it. Without them she's not sure where she'd be right now.

ALLISON MATALONE

Allison is a stay at home mom who, when not getting puked on or picking up kids from school, likes to stare at a computer screen and occasionally put her thoughts down onto a document. She hopes to eventually produce something substantial.

Also she loves her husband, Daniel, and sons: Dominic, Vincent, and TBD.

ROCHELLE SANGABRIEL

Rochelle Sangabriel is a book coach and writer. She spends most of her time writing, critiquing her clients' work, or in pursuit of her other favorite things: books, dogs, coffee and chocolate. She lives near Dallas, TX with her husband and four children. Romantic suspense is her favorite genre but she also reads plenty of fantasy, contemporary, military and historical romance. You can connect with her on Instagram @rochelle.sangabriel or #everystoryneedsalittleromance.

K.I. RUNYON

K.I. is a Type A corporate fiend who never knew that writing was the creative outlet she needed. Despite never having written a single word before the COVID-19 pandemic, a chance encounter with the local library's writing group over zoom helped her realize there was a place for all those worlds she had built in her head at night. Her current work in progress is fantasy, and she hopes to publish that novel in the next few years. Karoline is married to a fantastic and wonderfully supportive human and is a devoted cat mom to Wallace and Bernie.

JILLIAN NETHERLAND

A Pennsylvania native who received her education in Rochester, NY, Jillian moved to Maine from Dallas, TX in August 2020, and never knows how to answer the question, "so, where are you from?"

Jillian is a nonprofit fundraising and marketing professional and enjoys live music, books, and creative writing. She is a regular contributor to a Maine regional quarterly lifestyle magazine called LA Metro and has had a personal essay published in the Publish Her Press anthology, Better Together. She resides with her husband, two young daughters, their dog, and a cat.

AMANDA KENNEDY

For years, Amanda avoided seriously writing by reading a small bookshelf worth of books on how-to-write. After finding a motivated and supportive friend to write with, she chanced upon a piece of Natalie Goldberg's advice in Writing Down the Bones; "to know some local people who are writing and whom you can get together with for mutual support." It was from this moment that the Kindred Writing Collective was founded. With her tribe of fellow writer friends, Amanda has written numerous short stories, entered several contests, begun work on her first novel and recently had an essay published in a Publish Her anthology.

Amanda teaches fitness classes, climbs mountains, loves intense conversations and quotes Natalie Goldberg like nobody's business.